Jeremy and the Gorillas

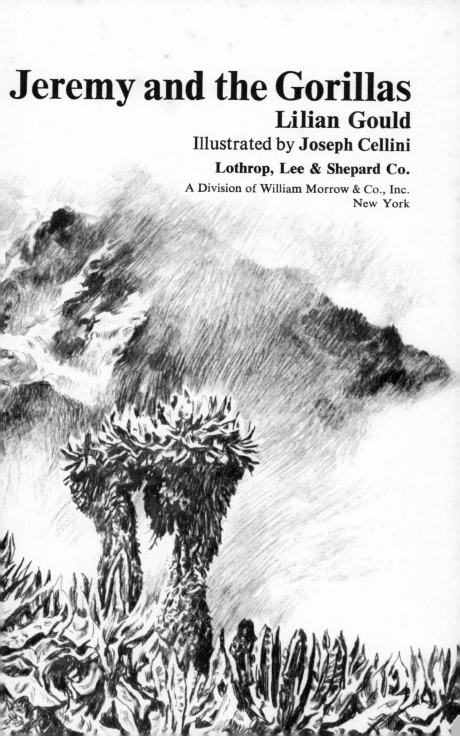

Jeremy and the Gorillas

Lilian Gould

Illustrated by Joseph Cellini

Lothrop, Lee & Shepard Co.

A Division of William Morrow & Co., Inc.
New York

1 2 3 4 5 6 7 8 9 10

Library of Congress Cataloging in Publication Data

Gould, Lilian.

Jeremy and the gorillas.

SUMMARY: After fleeing his home during a Mau Mau uprising, a young boy is accepted by a troop of gorillas living in the Virunga Volcanoes of southwest Uganda.

[1. Gorillas—Habits and behavior—Fiction.
2. Uganda—Fiction] I. Cellini, Joseph.
II. Title.

PZ7.G7348Je   [Fic]   77-589
ISBN 0-688-41803-1   ISBN 0-688-51803-6 lib. bdg.

Author's Note

This book owes a debt to
George B. Schaller,
for his gorillas
and to
Colin M. Turnbull,
for his Pygmies

Contents

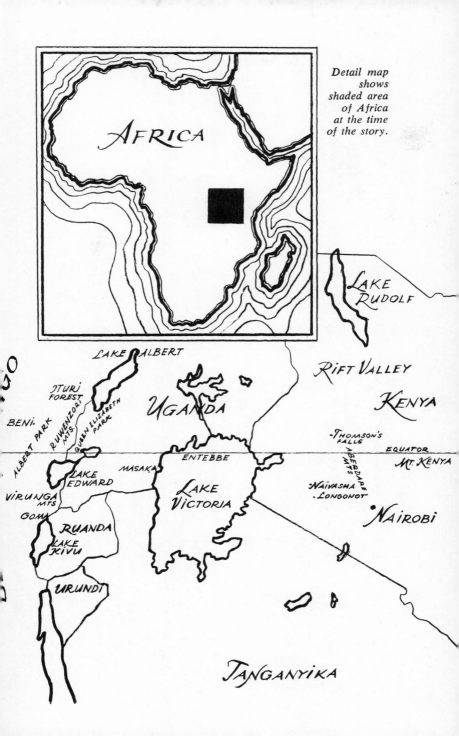

Chapter One

To Ride a Gorilla

One day Jeremy thought he was done for, that he would have to give up and go back to civilization. And because of such a silly little thing, too: a thorn in his foot. It didn't seem right after all he had been through.

He sat down on the warm grass alongside the buffalo trail that wound up and down the mountain, and rested his back against a tree whose ragged bark felt rough through his worn shirt. The spreading limbs of the tree sheltered him from the high equatorial sun which, at midday, could become intolerably hot. Propping his sore foot on his knee, he examined the nasty-looking wound for the hundredth time. Infected! He imagined blood poisoning, gangrene, amputation. "Blast!" he exclaimed aloud to no one, observing that only a simpleton would run around these woods barefoot. That is, unless he were a tough-soled African.

Back home in Kenya there was an old lion that had caught a mess of porcupine quills in its paw. That old lion was so mad from pain that Jeremy's father had to shoot it. Jeremy was that mad right now, but not from the pain. "The whole blooming thing's spoiled," he wailed. "Why in blazes can't I ever do anything right? I can't chase a hare if I have to hop on one foot. I'll starve up here!"

A moment later he was telling himself, No! Whatever happens, I won't go back; I jolly well won't. Shouldn't have thought of doing that even for a minute. If Father were here I know what he'd say:

J.J. you're nothing but a bloody quitter! Father always said that living isn't much different from facing a charging rhino. *Stand your ground, lad,* he said, *and make the whole bloody world swerve around you!*

Well, Jeremy thought, I guess if I had done that I wouldn't be here. He looked upward, half afraid that Father was watching him from heaven, and his attention was arrested by a bird that chirped like a squirrel. He reached for his bow, but before he got it strung the bird hopped along the branch and flew away.

Insects buzzed; leaves rustled in the breeze. Otherwise the forest was silent—and strangely mysterious, too, because of the way the glaring midday sun touched the forest floor at intervals between tree canopies.

Nothing to do but sit here, he thought, and wait for the gorillas to come back—if they do come back this way. He considered limping back to that clearing where he'd left his knapsack hanging along with his jacket and boots on the limb of a tree. Too far.

He regarded this wood where he and the gorillas had been living. It was like a two-story house, with an upper story of trees and a lower one of plants. The roof was a green canopy, the rooms the wide spaces beneath—a succession of clearings, each with its own individual dappled pattern of yellow-green light and

4

gray-blue shadow. The floor was this soft, springy grass he was sitting on while gazing upward at the green ceiling that was draped with moss and hung with lianas. His house.

This mountain forest was like a paradise because it received enough light and air for vegetation to grow in great variety. Even where the trees were largest, beams of sunshine filtered through, subdued to greenish tints. The altitude—much too high for most people —suited a highland dweller like himself. The climate suited him, too: crisp, cold mountain air and on a clear day, hot sun. It was balm for Jeremy's bruised mind just to sit in a golden shaft of sunlight, listening to the silence and stillness of the forest and knowing that he was finally safe. "Safe!" he said. "What if there *is* a leopard or even two of them on these slopes? At least with a leopard you stand half a chance; it's not treacherous the way people are."

There was a leopard on the mountain. On the way up Jeremy had caught a glimpse of a golden spotted hide sliding through dark green leaves. And there was the forest duiker that was being stalked by the leopard, its little head lifted in alarm, its tiny horns quivering. Then the delicate antelope had lived up to its name, which means "diver," by diving into the bushes.

Once he would have sighted that duiker with his rifle and shot it in the heart, quick and clean. Or even that leopard. But now he had no guns; only a sharpened stick that couldn't kill anything. He sighted down the length of the stick and pretended to pull a trigger.

Only a silly stick, a useless wooden spear with its sharp end hardened in a fire. The sort of thing a child plays with before he is old enough to be given a real spear. He balanced the stick above his shoulder and threw it. It fell with a soft clatter. He closed his eyes and visualized a seven-foot-long iron spear with a stout wooden handle: straight and true and deadly. Zing! Right in the leopard's throat so it wouldn't rip the flank.

That leopard would not have attacked him, but would only have defended itself if he came too close or if it was a female with cubs concealed in the underbrush. It is different with the black leopard, though. A trapper back home had told him that the black leopard has a taste for ape flesh and that it will tear into a gorilla troop, mauling and ripping the young gorillas. That would have to include me, too, he reminded himself, and giggled at the idea of the black leopard's not knowing the difference.

Shouldn't the gorillas be coming back? He kept his eyes on the trail made by the continual scuffing of the soft soil by the pointed hoofs of generations of black forest buffalo. It was upon this narrow trail that the gorillas had gone to forage, and he hoped it was the route they would follow in returning. Still, he could never tell about these gorillas. The path they followed was always determined by the leader, and it seemed to him that the leader of this group did not always know where he was going. Their wandering seemed a haphazard affair, like the route taken by a person shopping

6

in a general store: considering, picking and choosing, discarding, sampling a bit of this and that, browsing and nibbling and tasting, and even sitting down from time to time as if to think.

But, unlike people, the gorillas never forgot the time. Because it was now almost noon, and because the gorillas followed a rigid time schedule if not a certain path, they would be ready for naps.

While he waited for the crashing noises that would announce the troop's progress through the forest, he considered his great good fortune in having made his way to the Virunga Volcanoes. *Mfumbiro*: "the mountains that cook," the Africans called them. He chuckled, thinking: The joke is on those Bantu tribesmen who live at the foot of the volcanoes. They must have been around here for hundreds of years, cultivating the land all around these mountains. They must have been coming part way up the slopes to cut bamboo, but never would they come to this forest.

Afraid of it; scared to death. They believe in evil spirits and demons, and they're so superstitious they think an evil spell will be cast on them if they come up to these parts. One of them must have caught a glimpse of the gorillas, because they whisper about huge, hairy monsters that snatch a man from the trail, choke him, and drop his corpse out of a tree in front of anybody walking along the trail. The idea of these animals behaving that way made Jeremy giggle and hug himself with delight—for the more terrified the natives were, the safer he was.

Another local rumor was that bloodcurdling shrieks came from this forest, emitted by these same fearful beasts to warn away anyone who might dare set foot on these slopes. "Now, that part might very well be true," he said to himself, "because these gorillas want to be left alone. The same as I do," he added.

He had discovered that gorillas were better to live with than humans—gentle and peace-loving, and rather sweet, in a way. Humans, on the other hand, must have something wrong with them the way they act, because almost everywhere he had been since he left home there was trouble. . . .

There came the crackling sound of wild celery being trampled, of nettles and blackberry branches being ripped and broken. *Here they are!* And on the fresh mountain air was wafted a musty sweet-and-sour scent —the unmistakable odor of gorilla.

King, as usual, was first. Jeremy had named the big male King rather than Commander or General for several reasons. For one thing, this shaggy leader seldom commanded, but rather kept himself aloof from the doings of the little group. Also this gorilla was the father, the head of the family and the only adult male in it. Particularly, though, the name had to be King because of the high pointed bone that sat atop his rugged head like a peaked crown. King had the largest crest of all the gorillas. And he had a majesty about him, too; this great ape bore his huge bulk with a confidence that comes only with wisdom and many years of living. For King was old—how old, Jeremy could not say; but he was past his prime, for the hair on his back was frosty silver like the hair of an old man.

Behind King came the three adult females—one older than the other two, for the hair on her head was gray. Jeremy had named these females Queen One, Two, and Three. The oldest was Queen One, a gentle animal who, even though she was oldest, never imposed her personality on the others.

In contrast, Queen Two and Queen Three were aggressive. They looked rather alike and always stayed together, yet engaged in frequent brief, stimulating quarrels which always caused in King a flash of annoyance. These two, it would seem, were great friends.

The next gorilla to come into view was the one Jeremy called "the new mother": a young, timid female who had a tendency to whine. She had breasts full of milk for the new baby which she held to her chest with a big hairy arm.

The infant had spidery arms like a monkey, a little pushed-in face, toothless gums, and almost no hair. It was about two weeks old, having been born while they were all living in the bamboo forest, shortly after Jeremy joined the troop.

Before the baby was born, the female was not noticeably pregnant. All the gorillas had enormous fat bellies anyway. Then one morning it was simply there, wet and slippery, with a vacant unfocused look in its dark blue infant eyes, and its arms and legs flailing out of control.

The three older females had gathered around the

baby, chattering excitedly. King had regarded the tiny creature with some interest, and even put out a finger to touch it. But since then he had paid it little attention.

That day the troop did not travel far, but stayed around that area of bamboo, foraging in little circles. They sat in the midst of the brittle canes, peeling the tough outer layers of the stalks as though they were bananas, and dropped the peels on the ground in neat piles as they munched the soft inner shoots. The new mother had to peel the bamboo and hold onto the baby at the same time. Yet, Jeremy noted, no gorilla in the troop offered to share food with her. They never shared food.

Now the only ones left to make an appearance were the two youngsters, of identical size and with an equal amount of energy and exuberance. They were most likely the children of Queen Two and Queen Three—even though it was more often the aged female, Queen One, who looked out for their safety. She was the one who kept track of their whereabouts, which was not always easy, and generally acted as a nursemaid or governess for the two young ones.

One of the youngsters was now dashing along with its arms outstretched. It jumped on the back of the other one and the pair of them went rolling over and over in the grass, looking like two black furry balls. If they were not playing leapfrog they were playing follow-the-leader or king-of-the-mountain, or swinging on hanging lianas, or punching and tumbling together. It went on like that all day, as if their sturdy little bodies had a store of energy too big to be contained. Jeremy found himself continually entertained by their antics, and he sometimes felt like their older brother.

These two he had named Jack and Jill. Not that he could tell what sex they were—not at the beginning, anyway. But when he saw them for the first time they were walking upright, hand in hand—coming toward him up the slope of the mountain. . . .

How long ago was that? One month? Two months? No matter.

For what seemed like days and days Jeremy had been delirious with pain and fever—alone and lost in the bamboo forest. He had been wandering for who knows how long around the crisscrossing elephant and buffalo trails that twisted and turned and doubled back on themselves among the tall slanting stalks of bamboo. Finally he fell to his knees on the wet and slippery ground, vomiting and retching—his pained stomach trying to rid itself of the quantities of poison peas he had so foolishly stuffed into it. Then he collapsed.

Looking back on that awful time, he saw the woody maze of stems and leaves towering forty feet above his head, closing out the sky and allowing only dim translucent light to filter through. And he remembered his fears: that his body would be pounded into the ground by a herd of passing elephants, or that a prowling leopard would find him there on the leaf-covered earth,

11

or—anything. For he had been sure that he was doomed to die little by little in that twilight forest, and his body be eaten by hyenas.

Now, quite recovered and very much alive, Jeremy recalled the sensation of relief—of rescue—he had felt when he focused his aching eyes on the two short, furry figures of the little gorillas. It was his first glimpse of the mountain gorilla. But at the time—with the pain in his stomach and the ache in his head—his view of the two miniature apes walking hand in hand up the slope on their hind legs seemed a part of his delirium.

When Jack and Jill had caught sight of him they stopped their upward progress, stood still on their bowed hind legs, and simply stared at him, inspecting with their round eyes and curious gaze this strange creature lying huddled on the ground and making no attempt to move.

As for himself, he would always be grateful to those two youngsters for their childish trust in the unfamiliar animal they had found, and for their childish boldness in not fleeing from him at once with their little squeals of fear as he had seen them flee from most strange objects. Never would he forget his gratitude, his debt to them.

For it was the children who had accepted him first, the adults in the party being more cautious, more wary of approaching anything unknown. And more sensible, too; for how did they know that this odd creature carried no weapon and posed no threat to them? Jeremy could only suppose that, being something wholly new to these slopes—a not fully grown human—he did not arouse their fears. Besides, he was half dead.

The scene that had taken place in the gloomy bamboo forest on that day when he first encountered the gorillas—and they, him—was being repeated now. Here he was, again disabled by a foolish act of his own —this time, bounding along the forest floor barefoot. And here they were again gathering around his motionless form. But this time there was no sign of the timidity that usually caused these animals to clutch at one another's hair, or the agitation that always brought on screams. Nor was there any of that silent melting into the bushes which is the gorillas' usual method of flight. For Jeremy had become one of the troop.

As he looked at them this day he thought that these apes were the most beautiful animals in the forest— more beautiful even than the graceful golden leopard, because no animal has to fear them. And as they stood there with their clumsy, bloated bodies and their wrinkled black faces, he saw not their homeliness but the undeniably handsome blue-black hair, long and thick and glossy, that fell like full sleeves from their forearms and covered all but their hands, feet, chest, and face.

It was their faces he loved: shiny polished black with expressive wrinkles. The nose looked as if it had been bashed in, spreading the fleshy, rubbery nostrils. The noses were varied enough to give each animal its distinctive appearance. The mouth was enormous and contained four long, pointed canine teeth; and overhanging the eyes were great jutting brow ridges. And there was that cap of black fur, pulled low, giving an ominous appearance like one of those witch doctors who wear a black monkey-skin headdress. The hair on King's skull was stubby in the style of a crew cut, which gave him a jaunty air.

Yet, despite the jaws, the teeth, the brows, in those homely ape faces were the gentlest, warmest brown eyes in all the world of animals and men. Those soft brown eyes were like the eyes of a dog that Jeremy had once owned. It had been a wonderful dog, until it was snatched from the veranda of his house by a leopard, and it had the same eyes, except that gorilla eyes are not set in the sides of the head like a dog's but are as forward-looking as a human's.

Those eyes were disturbing to him because they were so expressive. With every passing emotion—curiosity, annoyance, anger, fear—those eyes would flicker, snap, flash, grow soft or hard. They could signal a silent reprimand with a hard, steady stare; they could register confusion, uncertainty, or dumb affection. Volumes of gorilla thoughts came through those eyes, and Jeremy was gradually learning to read them.

"It's a curious thing," he said to himself: "even though I haven't spoken to a human being in all the time since I came up this slope, I have never once felt lonely. Who needs talk, anyway? And who needs people? Sometimes when I was down there where it's

crowded with people I felt lonely; but never up here, never with the gorillas."

At the moment seven pairs of gorilla eyes were regarding him. The four females broke into excited chatter; for any break in gorilla routine, no matter how slight, is occasion for agitated ape conversation.

Jeremy pointed to his foot. King's eyes followed to where he pointed. But the look was quizzical, without comprehension. How could King know that a thorn imbedded in a foot hurt? King's own huge feet had soles like rhinoceros hide. How could King help, either? Look at those hands! Like a human's except for a shorter thumb—hands strong enough for breaking heavy branches or yanking roots out of the ground; gentle enough for touching an infant, skilled enough for plucking a leaf—but they were hands that never used tools.

The company was becoming restless. These gorillas had a short attention span, and their attention was already turning away from the unusual event. It was time for naps. The high sun was beginning to slide westward. They were sleepy, and not accustomed to such delay after their exhausting morning searching for wild celery and leaves and nettles to fill their bulging stomachs.

Jeremy stood up, balancing his weight on King's shoulder. Then, using the long hair as a handhold, he hoisted himself up the mountainous body to the immense rounded shoulders. From elbow to elbow this massive back measured five feet, which was almost

Jeremy's total height. He wrapped his thin, sun-browned arms as far as they could reach around the place where a man's neck would be, except that King's head and back flowed together in one great muscular mass, and he dug his bare toes into gorilla hide.

It was not unlike hanging onto the neck of his own tall, strong father who used to run round and round the big farmhouse with a much smaller Jeremy screaming "Giddyap" and digging his bare toes into his father's leather belt. It smelled different, though. Father always smelled of fresh air and hay and leather polish and clean male sweat all mixed together in a comforting aroma that could make you feel secure and protected. How Jeremy had loved those "horsy rides"! And how he would coax with his reaching arms to be lifted to those big shoulders where he could feel the muscles move beneath the rough khaki shirt. When he was bigger, Father had hoisted him up to the back of his own bay mare, but that was never as comforting.

"Forget that!" he ordered himself. "No good thinking about those other times, the good times. They're gone—everything's gone. This is your home now, this forest; and this is your family, these animals."

Sometimes he had to remind himself that they *were* animals. Their behavior often made him feel that no difference existed between them and himself. That was because they suited him. It was their gentle nature, their shyness; it found an answering response in his own nature which, he had already decided, wasn't suited to the violent confusion of civilization anyway.

17

When King stood, he stood tall on his short bowed legs: about six feet tall. And he must weigh, Jeremy estimated, over three hundred pounds, maybe four, with most of the weight in the shoulders and chest. He supported this weight on broad powerful arms that were so long they reached the ground when he was leaning on his knuckles; and he could run surprisingly fast on the flat soles of his feet when he used the knuckles of one big fist as a third foot. That was what made it such a rough ride.

The uneven, jerky, slantwise gait, leading with one shoulder and the face turned sideways, jarred Jeremy's teeth and took away his breath. King, who usually moved at a slow and deliberate pace, may have been trying to dislodge his passenger. It was hard to tell what went on in the mind of this unpredictable giant who was charging through the tall undergrowth of thistles and nettles that slapped Jeremy's face and left stinging welts. He felt a few more cuts and scrapes being added to the ones he already had as saplings whipped across his tightly closed eyelids and tugged hard at his tangled shock of matted hair.

The other gorillas were probably delighted to be finally on the move, because they squealed and grunted and bounced up and down as they followed in single file along the narrow trail, running at the same brisk pace.

For the apes this was a new game. If this was what King wanted to do, then it must be the thing to do.

The gorillas were funny that way: whatever King did, they did.

For Jeremy it was sheer excitement. "Wizard!" he exclaimed, thinking: If those chaps at the Nairobi Polo Grounds could see me now!

Chapter Two

King of the Mountain

Jeremy succeeded in curing his sore foot by burying it in the loose earth that was always moist from the mists and dews that lay upon the ground most of the day. He did this every afternoon while the gorillas rested. "There now," he said to himself, "there's no reason why a healthy person like me can't stay on this mountain forever." He had once read a book that described a tradition among the Australian aborigines. Australian boys no older than himself are made to prove their manhood by surviving for a full year in the wilderness. Alone, and supplied with only a knife and a bow (which were the only weapons he himself had), the boy is forced to live off the land. And that land is much harsher than this lush forest.

On one particular day the gorillas had chosen for their naps a little clearing in the forest where the tropical sun angled through the leaves of tall treetops. Here Jeremy was whittling away at a new bow he was making while idly observing the gorillas.

The four females were gathering sticks and leaves. The young mother, who never released her infant from her arms, had to do her gathering with one free hand, which meant many more trips for her. Every afternoon, and again at dusk, the apes constructed new beds—always in a different site. To Jeremy, this bedmaking never ceased to be intriguing.

Some beds were built high in a tree, some halfway down, others on the ground. The choice of location seemed to depend on the personal preference of the gorilla that intended to sleep there, or more likely depended on the animal's size and weight. For Jack and Jill slept high; the mothers slept lower down, with the baby in its mother's bed; while King, who never climbed trees, dropped some leaves and twigs in a heap and flopped down on the ground.

The females and children were quick and clever at bending the crowns of saplings, weaving the branches together, and adding a lining of leaves, using anything that happened to be handy. Jeremy had tried one of these beds for himself, first testing its strength the way they did, and then curling up in what looked like an untidy eagle's nest but felt like a springy mattress.

Since Jeremy found the soft ground comfortable enough for a daytime sleep, he wondered at the reason for the daily nest building. Whatever their reasons, this was the way the gorillas prepared for naps and again for the long night's sleep which lasted a full thirteen hours, from dusk until an hour after sunrise.

Thirteen hours is a lot more sleep than any human needs, especially if that human has had an afternoon nap. Jeremy always stayed with the gorillas during their nap time. During their morning and afternoon foraging trips he traveled with them. But his own early morning hours were spent quite unlike those of the apes.

After a sound night's sleep the gorillas always awakened sluggishly, rubbing their eyes and grumbling and grunting and yawning until hunger forced them out of their beds. Not until the bright sun pressed upon their eyelids did the first gorilla stir; and even then they all had to wait for King to get started, which he did with reluctance.

Because the gorillas were late sleepers and slow starters, Jeremy was able to use the early morning hours for his secret pursuit. It was secret because he did not want the gorillas to see him hunting. They would not understand the killing. Were they to see this creature whom they had befriended snatch a small animal, crack its skull with a rock, and slit it open with a knife, they might flee from him in fright. And he needed them more than they needed him. He was constantly worried lest by some action of his own the apes should recognize their companion as one of their enemy species. What if they suddenly realized that they were harboring in their troop one of those creatures known as Man the Killer?

These volcanoes and the land around them were the part of the continent most recently penetrated by Europeans. Jeremy imagined what it must have been like fifty years before, when the first white man walking through these mountains had spotted a group of huge, hairy apes climbing around the slopes. The man would have shot them, of course. And it would not have been long before other men came, bringing high-powered elephant guns.

Putting together what scraps of information he had, Jeremy proceeded to calculate that because this section of Albert Park had been set aside as a gorilla refuge only twenty-odd years before, and because gorillas are supposed to live to twenty years or more, the oldest apes here could have heard a gun fired in these mountains—could even have witnessed the shooting of a gorilla. Would an ape remember? Would it communicate its fear of guns—its fear of white men —to its children? Some animals are able to do that. Just to make certain that nothing would interrupt his happiness, that the apes would not expel him, he was careful to wash the smeared blood from his hands and face before he rejoined the troop.

Some of his early mornings were less successful than others, for game was not plentiful here as it was on the open plains of Kenya. And without a gun, without even another person to help, with nothing more than his bare hands, his bow, his wooden spear, hunting was hard work for the little amount of meat that could be gotten from this forest.

He tried not to let his mind dwell on the sleek bushbucks his father used to bring home and which the cook would roast. He tried to keep his mind off the good rich soup that was made from the bones and trimmings. Instead he would think of something small like a hyrax or a bird.

So he set out every morning to make his secret little

kill, to impale his meager catch on a stick sharpened at both ends, and to light his secret little fire, for which he employed the ancient African method of the fire drill. He twirled a stick rapidly between the palms of both hands as it rested in a notch on another stick held firmly by one foot. A puff of smoke; add a little dry moss, some leaves, blow furiously, and there is a flame. Thus he fed his craving for meat.

Sometimes as he crept through the underbrush, listening for the telltale rustle made by an active little animal, reaching into hollow logs, waiting beside burrows, he got the uneasy feeling that what he was doing was somehow wrong. Where, he wondered, did such a feeling come from? Here he was, a chap known in his neighborhood as the "little white hunter," starting to think of this hunting as murder. Perhaps that was because he had been living with no other companions than the gorillas, and they were strict vegetarians.

"I know why this hunting feels wrong," he said one day. "It's because I'm hunting without a license. That's called poaching, and where I come from everybody hates a poacher."

He remembered the anger he felt whenever he came across a steel wire snare set by poaching natives along the game trails or around water holes. But that kind of poaching—killing wild animals for their hides or tusks or horns—was different. It was big business in Africa, with a hundred organized gangs of Africans involved in it.

Those Africans. They used to be great hunters. Now

they are nothing but great killers. Jeremy thought of the animals he had seen with legs torn from their bodies, dying an agonizing slow death from infection and fever, waiting for the vultures or the maggots. What a waste! A single hunter, a single spear, even a single gun: that's nothing. But think of one snare catching, say, a hundred animals a day, including females and young which anybody knows shouldn't be taken. And those blasted poachers don't even go out to check their traps every day to see what's hung up in it, or what animal's leg is ripped.

Sometimes, when he was busily engaged in making more arrows, he would think about poison for the arrow tips. He never made any of the sticky black stuff, though. The Pygmies and the Bushmen brew poison from the seeds of a poisonous plant or they cook it up from the wood and bark of a tree. Those tribes that live strictly from hunting would have no meat without the poison that tips their arrows. But take those poachers, now. With their poisoned arrows they can take thousands of giraffes, rhinos, zebras, wildebeests, and elephants every year. Right in the big game reserves.

What a way to kill an elephant! The great beast goes lumbering and trumpeting off with that arrow stuck in him dripping poison into his bloodstream, and the faster he runs the quicker it works. Then he falls down. And what a terrible thing it is to see that elephant thrashing about in agony while the rest of the herd gathers in a circle around him. The Africans say that the herd knows when an elephant is hit by a poisoned arrow and are trying to prevent the poachers from cutting out the tusks.

Jeremy reminded himself that he used to dream of becoming a game warden, rounding up poachers and sending them to prison for two years. But now he said to himself, "There isn't a blooming thing a chap like me can do about the lawbreaking or the killing that goes on in the world. A bloody waste of time trying to change things. I have enough to do just taking care of number one, old Jeremy Jenkins here, and seeing that he gets something to eat."

Hunting always involves a lot more tracking than killing. And a good thing, too, he thought, because I was getting to be a first-rate tracker before all the trouble started and a fellow wasn't allowed to go off into the bush whenever he felt like it. "Well, my lad, you can put your tracking to good use because you're hunting for your life now; this isn't fun and games the way it was at home."

So he kept his wooden spear sharpened and its point hardened in the fire. And he kept his grim determination to pit his skills against the cunning of wily little forest creatures and come off with a satisfying breakfast.

He looked forward to his mornings. After he had been on the mountain for a number of weeks, the forest became as familiar to him as his home in the Highlands had once been. He came to love its wild beauty and its solemn silence. And so each dawn was filled not only with the urgency of his hunting but also with the pleasurable anticipation of exploring his forest until the sun broke across the horizon with a streak of orange-colored light. The time to start back was when the sun turned the hanging moss, called "old man's beard," to silver.

The silver color and soft texture of this softly hanging moss always reminded Jeremy of King's shining pelt, and of the day when he climbed onto that broad back for a ride: the day he was afraid he would have to chuck the whole marvelous miraculous thing that had happened to him. For it was nothing short of a miracle that he found himself living up here with wild creatures—the gorillas and the little animals whose lives he took only to sustain his own. It was as if God had reached a hand down from heaven, had plucked one terrified person from the midst of all those other terrified people, and had dropped him on this mountain. Of course, that was not how he had actually come here. But Father always did say that God works in mysterious ways.

Daily life had settled into a pattern determined by gorilla custom. Mornings were spent foraging. While the apes fed on wild celery and nettles, leaves and vines, Jeremy foraged for blackberries and roots. It was little, but if he had consumed even a small amount of meat that day it was enough to sustain him. While the gorillas got their water from their diet of leaves, his own water flowed clean and clear in the mountain streams. The only food he had in common with them was fruit and some tubers he dug with his knife.

Late afternoons, until sunset, the gorillas occupied themselves with a second feeding—less hurried than the morning meal—while he splashed in the cold water of a stream or kept the troop in view from a perch in the crotch of a tree.

Oftentimes he played with Jack and Jill, running downhill with arms outstretched, lying on his back doing bicycle exercises with them, climbing trees, or walking the way they did, stiff-legged with a bouquet of foliage balanced on his head. He had tried joining in their rougher games but had to give it up, because more than once his breath had been knocked out of him and his skin bruised by the impact of two muscular, compact bodies, each packing his own weight.

Between the morning and afternoon feedings the gorillas slept—all, that is, except Jack and Jill, who took this opportunity to play without danger of becoming separated from the adults. This was the time of day when the sun was at its hottest and brightest, and it was the only time that Jeremy was able to fall into a deep dreamless sleep.

That was the way it always was except for this one particular afternoon, which started out like any other with the gorillas getting ready for bed. Jack and Jill had climbed a tree and were sitting there with their legs dangling, waiting for their elders to get to sleep so they could wander around the prone bodies, playing follow-the-leader across outstretched legs and distended stomachs. These two youngsters were, at a guess, three or four years old, and still not as independent as they often pretended to be. They acted like an eight- or ten-year-old human, occasionally seeking comfort from their mothers when they were frightened or sleepy. If this had been a rainy day they would have napped like the others. But, fortunately, they were awake when the disturbance occurred.

There was King. He had lowered his bulk to the ground, swept a pile of leaves around his body, and stretched out on his back with his knees bent and his hands folded beneath his head in a posture so human that Jeremy could not help laughing aloud at him. King fell immediately into a deep slumber, with his fat belly thrusting upward like a beach ball. The three Queens slept each in her own bed which had taken a total of one or two minutes to construct in that skilled way they had. The females were sleeping on the ground that day.

The new mother was not as placid as the other females. Obviously a mother for the first time, she was always turning her squirming infant this way and that as if not certain just how it should be handled. She was much younger than Queens Two and Three, both of whom managed their children with an expert hand.

Jeremy regarded them: what a strange little family! One father, who, it seemed at the time, assumed little responsibility for a devoted family that never failed to follow where he led; two middle-aged mothers of children born at about the same time; one young mother who was unsure of herself; and one old female with wise, kind eyes to whom no one paid any attention, but whose glance he often found upon him when he chanced to catch her unawares.

Whenever he returned this glance, which seemed to be speculative, Queen One always dropped her gaze. But that, as he learned, was because gorillas hate to be stared at directly. They seem to feel that a stare is a threat. King made use of the stare to stop a quarrel between the females; the females used it to subdue the children. Jeremy knew better than to stare; the only glances he turned in their direction were stolen ones, like those of the old queen when she turned her contemplative watery old eyes upon him—as she was doing now.

The baby, clutched to its mother's breast with one shaggy arm, was feeding. When it finished it began to whimper in a very human baby way. The whimper became a high, thin wail; its eyes were squeezed shut, its arms and legs waving.

This happened all the time, and it made him uneasy. If King had been awake he would have been annoyed, too, and would have put out a hand to touch the unhappy infant. As it was, Queen One reached over from her bed as if to take the baby, or to retrieve it from where it was slipping down its mother's lap to her knees. But the new mother slapped the helping hand, pushed Queen One roughly aside, grabbed the anguished bundle of arms and legs and wide open mouth, and turned her back on the old one, curling up on her side and fairly smothering the baby in her huge arms.

At last silence reigned in the clearing, broken only by a few chirps from a tree frog and the chattering of a golden monkey, and, of course, by the vibrations of digestive stomach rumbles. Also by an occasional belch.

Then into this lazy quiet came the crackling and crashing noise of something barging heavily through the dense bamboo. What came there was not the leopard, who comes soundlessly, but a clumsy something that trampled and snapped the brittle stalks. It was not the sound of a buffalo, either, for that one takes the trail. And it could not be a troop of picnicking gorillas because bamboo shoots are available only in the rainy season; gorillas would not be feeding on them now. Besides, there were no other gorillas on this slope.

Jeremy's eyes strained through the confusing patterns of light and shadow that dappled the woods; through the tangle of leaves, creepers, lianas, foliage, in an effort to make out a shape of some kind. But there was nothing there except the stand of trees that edged the clearing.

Crawling cautiously on hands and knees, he made

his way to where King lay peacefully blowing air in and out of his fat, fleshy nostrils. He whispered in tones tense with urgency:

"King, for God's sake wake up! Something's coming up the slope."

King's eyes opened halfway, then closed again, having seen nothing more unusual than Jeremy.

He poked King in the belly, the shoulder, the cheek. It was like poking the earth. How soundly he sleeps! Jeremy thought. Not at all like other animals who have to keep alert for danger. Nothing would dare attack a gorilla except a leopard or a man.

Please don't let it be a man, he prayed. Anything but that.

Finally one of the louder and closer crashes must have penetrated King's consciousness because he sat up slowly—alert now, and listening. Was he testing his knowledge of forest noises, his experience of forest residents? Was he searching his dim memory for past occasions of intruders? Who knows?

Jeremy addressed the clearing: "What good will *he* be anyway?" He was thinking that King was no better at smelling out danger than he was himself. And the big ape was even less able to clamber up a nearby tree. So the two of them remained there, vulnerable, both relying on their keenest sense, their vision, which they strained toward the noise.

Another crash and King was on his feet, all knuckles digging into the ground, his massive head swiveling from side to side. His body and arms were stiff, and his eyes glinted with black sparks. Whether this expressed fear or anger was hard to tell, but he certainly looked impressive.

Finally there loomed into view a high gray shape. "An elephant!" exclaimed Jeremy softly. "Of all things!"

An elephant was the last thing he expected to see some ten or eleven thousand feet up on the side of a mountain. He had only seen them on the savannas and, in recent years, on the lower slopes of mountains where the natives had converted their range into cultivated fields. These animals need plenty of space, and grass; but here was this one plowing through a thicket of bamboo, looking as awkward as if it were stumbling through a roomful of delicate chairs.

It did not see them at first, but came laboring up the slope with its vast ears flapping in slow rhythm with its uphill progress, its long trunk swinging from side to side with each heavy step and its little triangular mouth keeping time with a sidewise motion.

It was a big old bull with, he calculated, at least eighty pounds of ivory in each tusk, because you figure that an elephant grows ivory at the rate of a pound a year. Wizard! It's a wonder some ivory poacher hasn't got this sour old outcast by now.

For it was obviously a deposed leader that was finishing out its days in solitary roaming—feet sore, teeth aching, temper vicious. Perhaps ants up its trunk. Watch out for this one!

When, at twenty paces, the elephant stopped and

trained two mean-looking little eyes upon the scene of sleeping gorillas, Jeremy kept his gaze steadily upon the ridged muscular trunk and the floppy ears. If that curving trunk should reach skyward, if those twitching ears should swing forward, somebody was going to get gored.

The look of this old rogue elephant was one that he knew. He had seen it make strong men run toward their Jeeps and their Land-Rovers, screaming to the driver to start the motor and go like blazes; because an aroused and charging bull elephant will overturn an automobile as if it were a bale of hay. And nobody has figured out what arouses an elephant's fury.

While the minutes passed, with two pairs of astonished primate eyes locked with one pair of nearsighted elephant eyes, Jeremy cursed his lack of weapons: With my father's double rifle, and at this range, I could get this big bull right in the earhole. Even if I still had my own guns . . . Curse my rotten luck!

Meanwhile, King had his own way of dealing with intruders that disturbed his nap. He roared. With his cavernous mouth wide open, he lifted his great black head and let out hoots and howls, screams and shrieks, that resounded for miles and sent back echoes. His long, pointed teeth glistened black with their coating of tartar. The sudden exposure of those knives in the usually serene face gave King such a ferocious look that Jeremy suddenly understood why the natives fear the gorillas of the volcanoes. The screams alone were enough to weaken the strongest of men.

King was only getting started. He beat his chest: rising to his full height on his short bowed legs, he bent the elbows of his massive arms and thumped his cupped palms on the bare place on his chest above the bulge of the belly. The sound—*pok-pok-pok*, like a slow tattoo on a jungle drum—was terrifying. Even the elephant was impressed. Stopping trunk and ears in mid-motion, that animal became as immobile as a gray granite statue.

The awesome exhibition of sound and fury was not over. King let out another roar that set all the wildlife scurrying, flying, fleeing. And he beat harder and faster upon his chest.

The hooting and chest-thumping sent the children hurtling down from the tree, scampering along the ground to clutch at their mothers' knees where the females were locked in an embrace of panic.

"Now I see it!" Jeremy realized that King's demonstration was intended not only to intimidate the elephant, but also to signal his family to run while he held the animal at bay. And run they did—crashing through the underbrush, diving into the forest.

When they were gone, King brought both arms backward behind his head, swung them furiously forward and down, slapping the ground hard with the palms of his hands. Then he drew himself up again to his full height and took a few quick steps sideways. Next he grabbed a handful of leaves from his bed and tossed them into the air. Splendidly standing his ground with all knuckles digging into the earth, he glared at the elephant. Finally, as if to settle the matter once and for all, he did a curious thing: he reached out, gently plucked a leaf from a tree, and placed it daintily between his lips. With that he pulled up tufts of grass and threw them into the air.

It was like a person snapping his fingers at a situation no longer important, except that King's eyes retained their fury and he did not turn his face from the elephant, which had stood immobilized during the entire performance.

The contest ended when the elephant turned its head. The trunk lowered, drooped; the ears relaxed. With a deliberate motion the elephant turned its body ponderously, presented a high dusty rump deeply wrinkled like loose trousers, and, with its little tufted tail swinging stiffly, slipped and slid down the brushy slope with a great crashing and crackling of vegetation. The sounds faded away in the distance; then, silence.

"Wizard!" Jeremy exhaled the word on the breath he had been holding. There flashed through his mind a picture in the Sunday school book: the one of little David slaying big Goliath. He turned to stare at King with admiration.

King, obviously pleased with the way things turned out, used his leftover anger to pluck a few more leaves and toss them. Finally satisfied, he sat down and crossed his arms over his chest.

On an impulse, Jeremy threw himself down next to the great body, closed his slender arms around one broad hairy arm, and buried his face in the dense pelt. He did not mind the smell: the musty, sour, wet-dog odor of an aroused male animal. On the contrary, he liked it; it meant security and protection.

The females and youngsters were standing tentatively at the edge of the clearing, peering around it nervously. And Jeremy generously included them, too, in a burst of gratitude for being permitted to share a mountain with such noble creatures.

It was a trivial incident—that is, in retrospect. Also, in the world of gorillas, it was a commonplace occurrence: that hooting and chest-beating upon the occasion of an intruder. This, Jeremy found out some months later. And he found out, too, that King, whom he thought to be the greatest of all gorillas, was an ordinary male gorilla, not as bright as some, not as young as most. In addition he learned that this little band of oddly assorted and totally isolated apes was not the most successful gorilla group on these mountains. But to Jeremy these animals were family: the only family, he told himself, he would ever want no matter how old he became.

When the troop settled down, and as Jeremy lay on the ground curled up alongside the bodies of the relaxed and sleeping apes, he made a promise to himself. He promised himself that he would never go back to the place he had come to call "The Valley of the Shadow of Death."

Chapter Three

The Shadow of Death

Night falls swiftly at the equator, and when it falls on the Virunga Volcanoes a sudden damp chill spreads like a moving shadow down from the cold summits. High up where Jeremy lived the crisp air turns frigid and the ground temperature lowers to freezing. Even before the fading of the afterglow the gorillas were always in their snug beds, curling up on their sides and making soft little humming noises.

By watching these apes construct beds twice a day, Jeremy had devised his own copy of a warm above-ground sleeping place. It took him longer than it took even the slowest gorilla, and his hands were not strong enough to bend springy sapling branches the way they did. But in ten minutes' time he managed to fashion a platform between two low horizontal limbs of a hagenia tree and pad it with leaves. Here he spent countless restless hours each night.

Only at night did the bloody corpses come to stand between him and the forgetfulness that would heal his mind. Those images, he told himself, arrived at his bedside by way of the Southern Cross that stood above his sleeping tree. For he seemed to remember having been told that each star in the sky is the dwelling place of the soul of a dead person, and this heavenly star arrangement was the same one that looked down on the Highlands of Kenya where tens of thousands of souls had been sent to wherever souls go when people kill one another.

The nights were not only dreadfully dark but dreadfully long here where there was neither lamp nor campfire. And since an equatorial night is twelve hours long, there was too much time between bed and sleep—too much time to lie on his back and stare into nothingness.

Several times his sleep was shattered by a scream of terror which caused him to start awake in a cold sweat. When that happened he told himself that the shriek came from a hyrax, whose nocturnal cries sound almost human. But he would awaken in the midst of a blackness more terrible than the blackness of the night. Finally, after Jeremy had spent a hundred sleepless nights in trees, he tried permitting himself to look into that terrible blackness for the first time. . . .

One night when the moon was rising low in the east like an orange lantern he allowed his thoughts to turn in that direction, toward Kenya. If he were a bird, or if he suddenly sprouted wings, he would point his feet to where the sun had dropped below the horizon. He would soar due east on a line parallel to the equator and one degree south of it. This would take him over the middle of Lake Victoria and into Nairobi.

Nairobi. That was one city he wished to avoid. He remembered the last time he was there with Father. Troops were patrolling the streets, army tanks were rumbling along Government Road, and natives were shooting one another in the alleys of the native quarter.

In Nairobi, men like Father—their sunburned, squinty-eyed, weathered faces looking grim beneath their broad-brimmed planters' hats—were striding through the lobby of the New Stanley Hotel or sitting on the veranda of the Norfolk Hotel, or gathering at the bar of the Equator Club the way they always did; only now they all wore holsters with a pair of pistols sticking out of them so everybody would see that the settlers intended to take care of themselves. And the settlers slept with those pistols, and a couple of shotguns, too, in their beds—with their finger on the trigger and the safety catch off. Even the women wore pistols in Nairobi; and when they dressed for dinner they all carried little revolvers in their handbags. It got so you didn't even want to go to Nairobi anymore.

If he were a bird soaring due east he'd rather land in an area called "Kikuyu country." It is a Kikuyu reserve, set aside by the government for that tribe, with a few white farms here and there, but mostly Kikuyu shambas: natives' farms of spiky pineapple plants and fields of maize. There are banana trees, and yam vines growing close to the little thatched huts that have smoke from cooking fires rising out of holes in their roofs. All neat and tidy and peaceful.

He would be among the rich, loamy slopes again, among the black fir and tall cedar trees where there are meandering rivers, twisting streams, and cool, mossy dells where fig trees grow.

His own farm was—or, rather, it used to be—just

the other side of Kenya's Great Rift Valley in a beautiful area of steeply sloping ridges laced with streams and rivers. Because this is the most productive land in Kenya, it was the place where the English colonists settled upon vast farms during the first few decades of the century. This was the spot in Kenya Colony where the English found a climate and a terrain that reminded them of home; where they carved out of the savage land of Africa a little bit of England: shooting, riding to the hounds, breeding fine cattle, and living in the manner of the landed gentry back home. Called the White Highlands, or "white man's country," Southwest Kenya became as British as England. And it bred people like Jeremy Jenkins.

"Well now," Jeremy commented to himself, "that's a curious thing: here I am living in the middle of the Western Rift and I used to live on the edge of the Eastern Rift." He was visualizing the way that big trench separates into two arms below Lake Victoria and curves up around each side of the lake as though embracing it. The coincidence gave him immense satisfaction because it meant that he had found a second home similar to his first home, and equally wild and beautiful, high and cool, rugged and mountainous— even the same distance from the equator.

But was it coincidence? He gave that some thought. Not really. Fate must have intended me to come to this place, he decided with finality. For Jeremy held the secret conviction that all events are preordained— at least those that concerned himself. It was a philosophy he had borrowed from the fatalistic Africans who, unlike Europeans, humbly resigned themselves to whatever might happen.

Having concluded that a benign fate had placed him on this mountain, he felt confident enough to peer a little further toward his past.

Still clinging to his fantasy of returning to the Highlands in the guise of a bird (it was not only easier and faster but, if you were Jeremy Jenkins, a lot safer than appearing there in person), he saw himself perched on a ledge of the Rift escarpment at a certain spot he knew well. From that high point even human eyes can see in one panoramic sweep for more than a hundred miles.

He saw it in his mind: About thirty miles from Nairobi is this place where Father always stopped the car and got out. . . .

Now the memories were coming back: the good memories.

Whenever he and Father went to the city to renew a hunting license or to pay back a loan at the bank, they always spent the day there. Jeremy enjoyed poking around the Indian bazaars and investigating the smelly alleys of the native quarter, which were a maze of rickety tin shacks.

Father, who always had a lot to do in Nairobi, could be found in the late afternoon on the veranda of the Norfolk Hotel, talking to the other English farmers about crops and weather and cattle diseases and blights and guns and such things as their daily lives were based on. In recent times, though, the men were concerned less with crops and weather than with the uprising, which had gotten out of hand. Jeremy would listen while he drank his lemonade, and the men often addressed remarks to him because it would not be long before he himself was a farmer, sitting around the Norfolk discussing crops.

Then he and Father would start for home. And where you can see the old volcano, Longonot, glowing in the setting sun Father would stop the car and say:

"What more could a man want? Lions to the south of me and elephants to the north. When God heaved up Africa and cracked it open, He pushed up the most beautiful country in the world: the Highlands of Kenya. There's no finer climate, no finer soil anywhere. It only wants taming, that's all." Then Father would say, "What a challenge! What a job for a man! Right, J. J.?" And he would stare for a long time at the golden grasses in the valley and at the sunset colors on Longonot. After that they would drive in silence toward home, going down into the valley and then crawling up the mountains to the cool high country.

Long before they got there they could see the jagged white peak of Kerinyagga. The white man calls it Mount Kenya and it fills the sky.

The great snow-covered mountain is an old volcano that rises from low green hills like an immense guardian angel seventeen thousand feet tall. And when Jeremy and his father finally arrived at their sprawling stone house, smoke would be coming out of the chimney because dusk brings a sudden chill to the Highlands.

The Jenkins farmhouse was long and low, with a thatched roof. Backed up against a low hill, it always looked to Jeremy as though it were kneeling to the majestic peak of Kerinyagga with its forehead on the ground and its arms outstretched—not the way the English knelt in church, but the way he had seen the people who came to Kenya from India worship their god after they closed the shutters on their shops.

The god that sat atop Mount Kenya now was the white Christian God, but it had not always been that way. Before the British came to Kenya, the Kikuyu tribe owned all the land on this side of the mountain. Their Great God Ngai, who sat atop Mount Kenya, gave it to them.

Ngai shaped the whole world around the mountain Kerinyagga. Ngai created the first man and the first woman "Gikuyu," and from their union came all the important people in the world who owned all the land on the fertile side of the old volcano. This was the story Jeremy heard many times when he was growing up, for he always played in the compond of mud-and-wattle huts of the Kikuyu who worked for his father.

Jeremy learned that before the British came, the strong brown-skinned Kikuyu raised their crops, tended their goats and cattle, and made war regularly on their neighboring enemy, the Masai.

The Masai were taller than the stocky Kikuyu, more beautiful, finer of feature, and shades lighter of skin.

But, as the Kikuyu pointed out, the Masai were no more courageous than the Kikuyu, no more fearless in battle than the Kikuyu—even though the Masai *were* a tribe of lion killers, and even though every Masai moran, or warrior, *had* killed a lion with only a knife and a spear before he was fully a man and a junior moran.

It was the long-standing tradition of these two East African tribes to launch surprise raids on each other in which warriors speared one another and carried off cattle and women and girl children to their own land. It was the custom—but no more. The tribal wars were ended when the British came and passed laws making it a crime to wage tribal war, and making it a crime for Kikuyu to spear Masai over the question of who owned all the cattle in the world.

Stories about the brave exploits of Kikuyu lapsed into legend when the British took from both the Kikuyu and the Masai their deadly seven-foot-long iron spears which were the mark of every senior moran. Also the five-foot and six-foot iron-tipped spears that were earned over the years as a youth matured from junior moran to senior moran. The British took the buffalo-hide shields, too, bleached white in the sun and handsomely decorated with tribal patterns.

The bwana Jenkins ruled over his Kikuyu workers —his "boys"—like a stern father over his children. He paid them wages and gave each man a piece of land on which to build a big round hut for himself and a big round hut for each of his wives. For a wife is never permitted to enter the hut of a husband. The bwana gave them land enough for each wife to farm her own section; and the food she grew went to feed all the family including the girls, who lived in their mother's hut, and the boys, who lived in their father's hut until they were old enough to go into bachelor houses and become circumcised and then move into their own houses.

Jeremy learned to speak Kikuyu when he was learning to talk. He practiced throwing a spear long before he was given his first rifle. He lived more in the compound of thatched huts than in his own house. He was, in fact, as much Kikuyu as he was English, the only difference being that he was the little white bwana who would someday be the big white bwana. But now, after what happened on the Jenkins farm that night, such a thing would never come to pass.

Now, at night, when Jeremy lay on his platform between two outstretched arms of a hagenia tree while the gorillas slept their deep untroubled animal sleep and the Southern Cross moved across a velvet sky, the corpses came to stand beside his bed like restless ghosts.

They seemed to be asking him to find a reason for the killing. His father was asking him, and so were the other English farmers and their wives and their children. The Kikuyu were asking him, too, because they knew that he was as much Kikuyu as English. It made him wonder if he was supposed to sort it all out in his mind so that he could tell them the answer.

It was as if they would not let him sleep—would not themselves sleep, either, but would keep coming, pointing at him with empty sleeves, staring at him with empty eye sockets, speaking to him with soundless lips until he did what they wanted him to do: *Look, Jeremy, look at it!*

The murders and the atrocities, the burning and the destruction, the horrors too awful to think about, the nightmares he lived with, were called simply "Mau Mau." The very words were enough to strike terror in a person's heart.

Mau Mau meant the swish of a panga: a big, curved, cane-cutting machete, heavy as an ax and sharp as a razor. Mau Mau meant the thrust of a simi: a short, double-edged stabbing sword. Mau Mau meant a spear through your back if you were foolish enough to turn your back on a Kikuyu, because no one knew which of the Kikuyu were loyal to the English farmers and which ones were secret members of the terrible Mau Mau group that had arisen within the Kikuyu tribe.

Mau Mau was a blind and bitter uprising against everything British, and already it had caused the slaughter of thousands of Kikuyu and hundreds of English farmers—including Father.

To Jeremy, Mau Mau meant more than the fear of a black shadow on the living-room wall. It meant the charred body of his father lying at the foot of the broad steps of the big veranda that ran the length of the farmhouse. *Look, Jeremy, look at it now!*

It was the day everybody dreaded; the day they

had guarded against, prepared for: the day the Mau Mau struck the Jenkins farm. Or, rather, it was the night, for the Mau Mau struck only under cover of darkness. And theirs was always a surprise raid, like the surprise raids the Kikuyu and the Masai knew so well how to launch upon one another in their theft of cattle and women and their slaughter of men and boys. But the Mau Mau took no captives; not even the animals were spared.

That night Jeremy was not where he belonged. He should have been at his father's side where lay the twenty-gauge shotgun and the two thirty-eight-caliber pistols. And every night since Jeremy had come to these mountains, his rest had been broken and his dreams haunted by the thought of how desperately Joe Jenkins must have fought to defend that farm which was his whole life. And defend it alone!

That farm was bought, as Jeremy well knew, with far more than money, which was hard enough to come by. Joe Jenkins left England, came to Kenya, and bought that farm bit by bit over the years with the strength of his back and the strength of his hands and his will to succeed in this British colony on the bulge of the earth.

Father always said that he had tamed a savage country even though he never succeeded in taming its savage people. He certainly tamed the soil, making it produce for him as it had never produced for the natives. And he liked to tell about the early days and the hard times he went through when he was trying to save his farm from the hands of the bankers, and of the troubles he had with crops and weather and climate and disease.

Joe Jenkins went down more than once before he went down for the last time on the veranda of his house, his head severed from his body with one swipe of a Mau Mau panga.

Before Jeremy was born, Joe Jenkins went down under a plague of locusts that wiped out every growing thing on the farm. He borrowed more money, but the tsetse fly came, bringing sleeping sickness to kill his oxen and cows and horses. Then came the war. Those hard years were suddenly over because the British needed more meat and more of everything, and the farm was producing beef at high prices. In his new prosperity, Joe Jenkins was able to build that big new house in which Jeremy was born.

It was the same with all the settlers. Houses like the ones Jeremy knew came later to the colonists. Those pioneers who came out to Kenya Colony in the early years could not afford four big bedrooms with bathrooms inside the house and water running through pipes. Their profits always had to go into the farm. It took a man thirty years to get where Joe Jenkins got.

Many of the English gave up and went back home, and a lot of them died there in Kenya, as Jeremy's mother had died, of the sickness, or a sadness, or maybe of overwork. Some of them committed suicide.

Jeremy knew the story by heart, and he had seen that every farm in the Highlands had on it many graves. But the trouble is, he thought, I also know the story of the Kikuyu, even though I do not see their graves because the Kikuyu put their dead out for the hyenas to devour. It is the custom.

Of the ghosts that came to Jeremy's bed carrying in their arms their severed heads, some had skins of suntanned white and others had skins of dark brown or black. He knew all of them as friends. Yet he knew them, too, as people very different in the way they did things.

For instance, the English never understood witch-craft, or the power of a spoken curse, or the influence of evil spirits, or any of the other things that regulate the daily life of a Kikuyu. On the other hand, the Kikuyu never understood the British making a law against the killing of Masai while at the same time they themselves were waging a big war overseas with an-other tribe.

But the misunderstanding was even bigger than that. It seemed as if the white Christian God was saying one thing while the Great God Ngai was saying another, with neither god understanding what the other said.

The trouble, of course, was over the land. Because the English paid money for it they thought they owned it. But how could the English own the Highlands when Ngai gave the Highlands to the Kikuyu tribe to use forever? And the tribe, as everyone knows, includes all the unborn children as well as all the dead ancestors. A misunderstanding. A mistake. And because of the mistake the Mau Mau took up up simis and pangas and swooped down upon the white farmers and their families and murdered them.

At first there were only occasional killings. Then the killings suddenly got worse, with almost every morning bringing its grisly news by way of the police or the wireless: another English family wiped out; cattle killed; grazing land burned. There were routine roundups of Kikuyu tribesmen; there were hundreds of arrests. There were interrogations that, some said, involved torture. There were a lot of jailings and executions. But nothing stopped it. That was because, if a Kikuyu worker was loyal to his *bwana* and his *memsaab* and the *kidogos,* he knew nothing that he could tell the authorities. If he was not loyal, then he would not talk even on pain of torture. That was because of the oath.

The police found out about the oath-taking. The oath was to kill every European in Kenya, and the Mau Mau wanted every Kikuyu to be sworn to the oath. If any tribesman refused to swear, terrible things happened to him—or they happened to one of his children while he was forced to watch.

The oath was black magic. And it was a blood oath, the kind used in the old days before the missionaries came and stopped it. The difference, though, was that for this oath they did not use the blood of a goat, which was traditional. To give this oath more importance, they used human blood. And they did not just sprinkle the blood in a circle; they drank it.

To become a member of the Mau Mau, a person

"drank oath." He swore to help in the killings and he swore not to inform on the leaders. The oath-taker's lips were sealed. A blood oath is so binding that a broken oath—even if nobody discovers it is broken—can kill the oath-taker. For the oath is magic.

That is why the farmers never could be certain which of their headboys, houseboys, cooks, farm workers, even their nursemaids, had been sworn into the fanatic organization. There were a million Kikuyu in Kenya and eventually ninety percent of them were sworn to help in the killings.

Every one of those murders of the English was arranged by the servants. The oath-taking magic was stronger than any loyalty to the white bwana and his family. It appeared that the god of the Christian missionaries had lost out to something that was there before they came to Africa. It was the old-time witchcraft.

Father said that the evil spirits of Black Africa were rising up from graves which were too shallow to contain them. That was his way of saying that the natives were only a few years away from being savages, and that the old superstitions still lived in the Kikuyu. He said that some smart leader had revived the old sorcery in order to wipe out all the whites.

What Father said gave Jeremy a guilty feeling. Having been raised in a Kikuyu compound while Father was busy running the farm, he could not help but absorb much of the lore about evil spirits and evil spells and the powers of black magic—enough to half believe in it. Secretly he felt like a white Kikuyu, more in sympathy with the belief in witchcraft than with the missionaries who tried to cast it out. In the beginning he felt confused.

Suddenly, though, his mind was made up. That was when the Mau Mau struck the farm of their good friends a mile up the road . . . burst in on the family while they were at dinner, strangled the wife in front of her husband's eyes, hacked the baby in its crib, and dragged the farmer away. Five weeks later the man's body was found; he had been buried alive in the forest near one of the Mau Mau hideouts.

August, September, and October were the most frightful months. In the space of three weeks forty-three English—men, women, and children—were butchered by the terrorists, who always left at the farm a sign in the form of a disemboweled cat or dog suspended from a fence post. But no sign was needed for the police to know who burned those acres of crops, who slaughtered those cattle, who wrecked that farmhouse and left lying on the living room floor in a river of blood what was once a living family.

By October most of Kenya's blacks were at war with Kenya's whites. A million against only a few thousand. And to Jeremy it was a far more terrible war than the one that had been fought overseas—the one into which he had been born.

For this was a war of secrecy and stealth, a war in which a door is thrown open by a fanatical murderer swinging a vicious blade at the terrified occupants of

54

a farmhouse nestled in some dark and isolated hill. It was a war in which you never knew whether the cook in the kitchen had just been hacked to death or whether he had unlocked the back door for Mau Mau conspirators. Even when you went to the bathroom at night you took your gun with you, and you only hoped you had a chance to use it before they got to you. Because you didn't want to be like that fellow who was hacked on his way to the outhouse, or the one who got it in the bathtub, or the woman who was only crossing her hallway to look at her baby. . . .

Living like that made a chap grow up in a hurry, made him tough and suspicious and wary of everybody around him—even of the gentle houseboy who used to tuck him into bed and sing to him the songs taught to the Africans by the Christian missionaries.

Why did Father and I think we would be spared? he asked himself. Was it because of the spitting? Everybody knew that soon after Jeremy was born three important Kikuyu elders came to the farmhouse veranda where he was lying in his pram; that they were dressed in their ceremonial feathers and headdresses; that each took a turn spitting into the baby's face, and then left. The bwana Jenkins and the memsaab Jenkins were pleased and proud because they knew what the spitting meant; knew that it is the Kikuyu tribe's way of welcoming and accepting a new child. Jeremy, being the kidogo of the respected bwana Jenkins, was blessed at birth by the Kikuyu, and was always a favored son of the tribe.

Then somehow it came to pass that, one night, the Mau Mau came for the heads of the bwana Jenkins and the kidogo bwana.

That night Jeremy was not at home but was out in the bush shooting something for the pot, accompanied by his good friend Njoroge—his Kikuyu brother, really, because the two boys had been raised together, first as babies in the big house, then more and more in the compound.

It was well known that the killers never launched a strike unless all members of the family were at home. If one of the family was away for the evening the raid was called off until another time. And this information was easily come by because every English household had its oath-taker.

But in the case of the Jenkins household, the very reliable informant (blast whoever it was!) must have failed to mention that the kidogo bwana was away. Or, more likely, that informant expected the boys back before dark. And they should have been back, too, because since the evening curfew the police sometimes shot first and looked afterward. For no one except the killers had any business being out after dark. It was only Jeremy's eagerness to bring back a Thomson's gazelle for Father that kept him out in the bush too long.

The vultures were already circling above the slaughtered cows when he got there. He remembers running through the pasture ahead of Njoroge, who was loaded down with the ammunition box, the shotgun, and the supplies. What else does he remember? Yes: there was something that someone had carelessly left lying at the foot of the veranda steps. It was a monstrous, mutilated almost-thing that he did not go close enough to see clearly. He didn't have to go closer. He *knew*.

There was also the body of a Kikuyu lying face down with a big hole in his back. Shot, most likely, by Father before those cutthroats jumped him from the rear and swung their pangas.

Njoroge was the one who turned over the body with the hole in it. Then he let out a high, despairing wail, his round face contorted out of shape and his big brown eyes bulging with the whites showing.

The dead Kikuyu was Njovu, Njoroge's older brother. And when Jeremy saw that, he knew why Njoroge cried out that way and why his frail black body was shaking with the same trembling terror felt by all the good people of his tribe when that happened. The family—the entire family—was cursed.

Quiet. No shots. No sounds at all except Njoroge's whimpers and little crackling noises coming from inside the burning house. No sound of barking, either: the dogs were dead, or else hung half-dead on the gateposts with their innards spilling out. Where were the guards assigned to protect the workers in the stockade? Run away, of course.

Now Jeremy saw it again: himself and Njoroge facing one another across the two bodies, flames casting an unreal reddish glow as if the scene were taking place in hell, and everything happening in slow motion.

Without realizing it, he must have swung the rifle from his shoulder while he was running across the pasture, for now he found himself gripping it in his hands, his finger against the trigger. That trigger was an ache against his knuckle; he felt the steel, and the feel of it made his body prickle all over. He had never before pointed a gun at a human being.

Now, one thing you could do was shoot Njoroge and then you could go on shooting Kikuyu until you got them all just to make certain that no Mau Mau remained on the farm. Easy. The guards had run away and no other Kikuyu except the thieving Mau Mau in their mountain hideouts had a gun or knew how to fire one. You could go to the stockade out back where the house servants and the farm workers were locked up for the night and you could use that rifle and that shotgun and that box of ammunition and shoot both guns hot. It would be like picking off a cage full of birds.

The other thing you could do was cut and run from the Highlands and keep on running until you came to some quiet place where you could stop running and think over the problem of what went wrong between the white Christian God and the Great God Ngai.

Chapter Four

Safari

Jeremy supposed that he was a fugitive now, for isn't a fugitive someone who runs away from the police? And he was being careful not to be seen by the African Special Police, the Police Reserve, the Kenya Regiment, the Home Guards, the Night Patrol, the Civilian Night Watch—*or* the Mau Mau. He knew too well what happens to a person who gets away from a Mau Mau strike. His throat tightened involuntarily where the knife would slide along.

How does it feel to lose your head? Does it hurt? How about being buried alive? Uhhgg; no thanks. Or having your hands or your ears cut off? Or your eyes gouged out? Thanks, but no thanks. I'll stay the way I am if you don't mind: all in one piece. Take care not to lose your head tonight; walk softly, he said as he struck through the low green hills, using the stealth of a hunted animal—which, he reminded himself, he was.

Listen! Was that an owl—or was it a signal? Was that a twig cracking behind him? A branch rustling over there? If only he didn't have to go through this cursed Mau Mau territory where those crazy cutthroats have their hideouts. But he had to in order to get where he was going.

Where could he go except westward? Eastward went

only to the ocean; northward went to the Northern Frontier District where only elephants and nomadic warring tribesmen lived; and southward was immense savanna, good only for hunting wild animals that graze in dry bush. For a terrified boy whose head was sought by the Mau Mau, the only course from southwest Kenya was the one Jeremy took that dark, moonless night known as All Hallow's Eve, a night when the evil spirits are said to walk abroad. But Jeremy knew that in his homeland in those days the evil spirits walked abroad every dark and moonless night.

In Africa, any journey is called a safari. And this was going to be the biggest safari of his life. The luminous dial on his watch indicated that there were several hours of concealing darkness ahead of him. His compass pointed the way westward, toward the country of Uganda. He knew there would be no problem crossing the Kenya-Uganda border. There were no customs posts there because both countries were administered by the British.

If you get mad enough you forget to be frightened, Jeremy observed as he pushed the miles behind him. Now that the feared thing had finally happened, he was feeling a curious lightness of spirit. Perhaps that was because he had been living through three years of dread and tension; of bolted doors and latched windows and drawn shades and closed curtains; of a rifle in his bed and two pistols on the dining table along with the food prepared by poor old Karinga who had to be herded every evening out to the stockade along with the farm labor and, for their own protection as well as the family's, locked up for the night.

The routine of daily life on the farm had become an intolerable series of meticulous precautions against sudden violent death. That, along with the heartbreak of watching the farm, with its unmilked cows and its untended crops, go to ruin while Father was off somewhere in the Aberdare Mountains hunting Mau Mau. Nor was there any labor to be gotten from neighboring tribes, either, for they, too, were taking the oath. Only the Masai kept clear of the oath-taking, herding their cattle as usual as if Kenya were not ablaze with hatred of black for white.

The war spread like wildfire, and the White Highlands became known as the "Bloody Highlands." Because now the Mau Mau had a supply of guns which they stole from gun racks in the farmhouses they burned. And they would kill anybody on the road for his gun, too, which was one reason Jeremy was keeping off the roads that night.

A state of emergency was declared in Kenya, and the British flew in a battalion of fusiliers from the Suez Canal Zone. But those soldiers were not trained to fight the kind of guerrilla warfare being fought in the Aberdare Mountains: the kind where a man's eyes are gouged out to make him talk, or his ears cut off, or his throat cut, but slowly. The soldiers did not even stop the Mau Mau from shooting their own tribesmen in the streets of Nairobi or prevent them from burning the Polo Club.

After a few years of fighting back, many of the settlers gave up, packed their things, put their farms up for sale, and headed for home or for Australia to try their luck at farming again. The Mau Mau had succeeded in their purpose: to "drive the foreigners into the sea." But some would not be driven. There were the stubborn ones like Joe Jenkins.

Pangs of guilt assailed Jeremy that his deliverance from daily terror had been bought with his father's murder. Still, he knew that such an end for one of the stubborn English farmers of Kenya was not unusual, and that Joe Jenkins could just as surely have met the same fate in the Aberdare Mountains where he and two thousand other volunteers went regularly to comb the hills, searching for the hidden caves and the secluded camps of the Mau Mau oath-givers, flushing out the treacherous runaway Kikuyu and trying to make them reveal the names of the leaders.

Whenever Father came back from his excursions into the mountains, filthy and exhausted, he would only sit and stare—and drink too much. He would ask Jeremy whether there had been any "activity" at the farm. Because several raids had been attempted and foiled by the ever watchful Kenya Police Reserve and the civilian spotters, summoned by shots from Jeremy's gun.

Father had long since stopped asking about the crops and the cattle. No doubt it was enough that his house was still standing and his son still alive. Then, after a hot bath and a long sleep, Father would clean his guns and go back to the Aberdares again to track Mau Mau and to do God knows what when he caught them. What awful things were happening up there in the cold and wet of the Aberdare forests Jeremy was never allowed to know because you had to be at least sixteen years old before you could join the volunteers. But he had reason to suspect that there were unspeakable tortures being used by the desperate farmers.

The last time he looked upon Father, that man, once so rugged and strong, had been reduced to a nervous wreck whose hands shook so that the ice rattled in his glass and whose eyes were glazed and bloodshot. All Father's dreams, thought Jeremy, have been shattered by the horror that calls itself Mau Mau. And the boy, as silent as the man, sat around the farmhouse which had become his prison now that the schools in Kenya were closed on account of what the British government called "the Emergency."

Joe Jenkins must have noticed his son's depression, his lack of activity now that he was not permitted to ride his horse; his lack of companions now that he was prevented from visiting the Kikuyu compound. That is doubtless why he suggested that little hunting safari with Njoroge. Njoroge was not only Jeremy's friend and gunbearer, but an excellent tracker as well.

Karinga the cook had little faith in the boys' hunting prowess—and a good thing, too, as it turned out. For the knapsack was stuffed with tins of tea and biscuits, fish, corned beef, beans, and a supply of biltong— narrow strips of meat dried in the sun. It was the contents of this knapsack, packed for a pleasure safari, that sustained Jeremy for the first several days of his westward flight.

Joe Jenkins had checked the contents of the ammunition box and had examined the two guns, cautioning the boys not to allow the guns to be stolen. For, as anyone knew, if you lost your gun, or even if you had it stolen, you went to jail for thirty days no matter who you were. Then Father embraced him, shook Njoroge's hand, Jeremy promised to bring back a Tommy—a Thomson's gazelle—as Father used to do in earlier, happier times, Father and son smiled at one another for the first time in months, and that was the end, the real end of life on the farm.

As Jeremy crept through the tangle of dark bushes on that moonless night of that last senseless slaughter in a long series of senseless slaughters, he knew that by now the authorities at Fort Hall, and soon those in Nairobi, would be wondering what had happened to him. They might assume that he had been hacked and his head carried off to be used as a gruesome trophy for public display atop a wooden stake in a Mau Mau camp. Or they would believe him to have been kidnapped, as so many were, to be used as a human sacrifice for the ceremony of oath-giving. Or, like the Chief of Police, who was waylaid on the road and his hands cut off, they might expect to find part of him tonight and the rest of him next week.

There will be the usual questions asked by the authorities. But Njoroge will tell them nothing because

64

Njoroge does not like authorities. They speak to him in Swahili: "baby talk." Some Kikuyu resent being addressed in a pidgin invented by Arab slavers, and all of them hate the Swahili tribe. Njoroge will speak only Kikuyu, and he will not speak of what happened back there.

(Poor scared little Njoroge with his skinny trembling legs and his big frightened eyes. Golly! the way he stood there with the shotgun strapped to his back and no idea of defending himself even if he had known how to fire the thing, which he didn't. Just waited to die, the way Africans accept dying. Njoroge knew how I felt when I swung that rifle toward him—like a wounded buffalo going straight for whoever happens to be standing in its path.)

No, Njoroge will not talk, because of what his brother Njovu did. Njovu had a hand in the killing of the bwana on whose shamba lived not only himself but his father and mother and brother and sisters. How the devil could Njovu raid the shamba of his own bwana? He knew his family might see him and identify him to the police. Then the Mau Mau would have to kill them all. Yes, that family is cursed, all right, and not only by witchcraft either.

For what was left of that night Jeremy walked the railroad tracks in order to avoid being seen by a police car, which was the only sort of vehicle allowed on the roads after the six o'clock curfew and before dawn. Then, as soon as the morning sun cast its dim light on the heavy cloud layer, he allowed himself to rest, his gun cradled in his arms because he was in the worst part of the Mau Mau belt.

For some time he had been conscious of the weight of the shotgun on one shoulder and the rifle on the other. Also the ammunition box strapped to his back. But he could hardly have left the shotgun with Njoroge, could he? It would be the same as leaving it with *them*.

"For all I know Njoroge's dead; for all I know everybody in Kenya is dead," he said. A lump came into his throat, and to loosen it he drank all the water in the flask and ate ravenously from several tins of meat.

Now that daylight had come he could, if he wanted to, go to the highway and flag one of those lorries that were heading into Nairobi with fresh provisions from the farms. He could see them from where he was: on a high ledge of the rift escarpment about forty-five miles north of the city. In less than an hour he could be in Nairobi where the police would look at him as though he had come back from the dead. They would question him about last night's strike on the Jenkins farm. Then, when he told them all that had happened there, they would assume he had walked all night just to get to the Nairobi police station. They would not know that he had simply bolted.

After the police station—what would happen next? The authorities would send a cable to his mother's brother who lived in someplace called Kent, and the next thing anybody knew, Jeremy would be on a ship heading for England.

"Hey! You'd better think about this very carefully," he cautioned himself. "What would you do in England? Wear a starched collar and go to an English school, of course. It will be worse even than the English school in Nairobi where they cane you for the slightest thing and make you learn Latin and sing hymns. So you'd better just hold up there, my lad, before you go flagging any lorries.

"Besides, I can't leave Africa. I was born here, which makes me part of this continent, like its soil. And I certainly don't want to be shipped off to a country I never even saw but only heard about from Mother. She said that in Kent the snow falls all over everything, right down to the grasslands, and the winters are freezing. But worst of all, she said that England has very few wild animals, and I need to be near animals—especially when everything gets all mixed up the way it is, and people act crazy, and it gets so you don't know who you can trust and who you can't."

That ended the argument. The matter was settled. Except for one detail, which he pondered, but not for long.

"Who needs school, anyway?" he asked aloud, smiling at the fact that even before the schools had been officially closed he could be found more often on the open plains than in the classroom.

Father only laughed about this. "We settlers," he said, "never claimed to be intellectuals. We're only plain dirt farmers, learning to cope with the bloody

African droughts and the pesky African bugs and the broken farm machinery that the boys never *could* learn to handle properly." With that, Father would give his shoulder a hard squeeze and say, "Get along with you, J. J., and mind you keep a sharp eye out for snakes."

"Right, Father," he whispered now to the lonely escarpment. And he touched two fingers to his forehead in a solitary little salute.

Down on the highway, the farm trucks were going by one after another, but Jeremy let them go and stayed where he was.

Later that morning he cocked a practiced eye at the sky and observed that there were fresh rain clouds banking up over the Ngong Hills. There would be another downpour before evening. Gathering up his heavy gear, he began the long hike through Uganda and toward that jumble of mountains that separate East Africa's high plateau from the Congo River Basin. He had no idea of what lay ahead of him, but neither did he look back.

Chapter Five

The Spirit of the Forest

At that time of year Uganda was a quagmire. It was muck and mud, marshes and bogs, with its dirt roads washed in streaming rivers of clay. Seen through sheets of pouring rain the landscape was monotonous farmland: fields of millet and maize, peanuts and cassava, and endless groves of banana trees.

The villagers fed him well and were friendly and hospitable, for hospitality is an African custom. Everywhere he went they offered him the best of whatever food and drink they had. And if the village was too small to afford a special guest house for visitors, the villagers cleared out one of their own houses where he could stay the night.

Although the natives of Uganda were accustomed to seeing Europeans, their sole contact with whites was with civil servants and Christian missionaries rather than with muddy English schoolboys dressed in bush jacket, khaki shorts, knee socks, and high laced boots. But since everyone in Uganda was aware of that thing called "the Emergency" in neighboring Kenya, and knew that the schools in Kenya were closed on account of it, they might simply have assumed that the English lad was on holiday. At least they asked no questions.

Because Uganda had been a British protectorate

69

since the 1890s, the official language of that country was English, which most of the natives had learned from the missionaries. But Jeremy found it easier to converse with them in Swahili, that mixture of Bantu and Arabic.

After Kenya, Uganda was wonderfully peaceful. Its British administrators had never permitted Europeons to own the land; no one but the native Ugandans could farm it. Therefore, thought Jeremy, no native uprising was likely to occur here.

He felt amazingly free: free to jump on and off a westbound train, or to catch a ride on a farm cart, or to ride along with a passing motorist whom he helped to get his car unstuck from the mud. He avoided the city of Kampala, slogging along the muddy unpaved roads instead.

In a town called Masaka he sold his watch, the one given to him by his father who had sent all the way to England for it. He did that in one of those little *dukas*, or general stores run, of course, by an East Indian. There were no other traders or any other kind of businessmen in Uganda except these Asians, descendants of people brought in to build the railroad. They owned every *duka* there, selling bolts of cloth, cooking pots, kerosene lamps, baskets, farm produce, and everything else that people need. In fact, there were far more Asians than Europeans in Uganda.

In return for the watch, the Hindu gave him some much-needed tins of sardines and meat as well as biscuits and chocolate. A poor exchange, come to think of it, but there was no meat to be had from the villagers, not even the well-to-do ones.

As for game on the hoof, the guns he carried were of no use to him at all. There was no longer a wild animal in all Uganda except in a game reserve or a national park. After Jeremy traveled almost all the way across Uganda he discovered that he had entered one of these parks. It was the Queen Elizabeth Park in the southwestern part of the country.

That was where it all began. He knew that later, much later, when he was contentedly settled in his mountain sanctuary and had a chance to reflect. In the Queen Elizabeth Park he was alone for the first time in his life, in a way he had never been alone before. Partly it was because this park was newly opened and was not yet supplied with roads. But even in an established park, visitors do not come in the rainy season because the game is scattered then.

There he was, looking across the grass and seeing no smoke from cooking fires, no car, no person, no sign of human beings. Only that westward extension of bright haze with cloud shadows being briskly wind-driven across a sea of grass the color of lion. A magnificent, mighty landscape that stirred only with wandering game: buffalo, wildebeest, antelope, elephant. He felt the peace of it—more than just peace: a sort of primeval calm as if humans had never come here.

"Wizard!" he exclaimed aloud to the stillness. "A chap could spend his whole life in a place like this. No reason why he couldn't."

Coming directly from the overcrowded villages teeming with humanity, this was like being hurled back in time. For grazing on the grass of the park and wallowing in the waters of Lake Edward were thousands of immense forms: the white rhinoceros, looking like something out of the last ice age—which they are. And because those rhinos and the hippos, too, could move surprisingly fast across the open grasslands, he held his rifle ready until he realized that no rifle was needed for protection here. The animals hardly noticed him.

He fantasized that he was Adam, with all the beasts being paraded before him by God. And, like Adam, he was giving the beasts names. Of course he gave them the names they already had—for those names suited them—but the diversion passed the time and the miles.

They say a man can walk at the rate of four miles an hour. If so, he could do twenty miles before his midday meal. But when Jeremy came upon a herd of about fifty elephants, cows and calves, he moved along with them at their ponderous elephant pace. They trod with quiet steps, deliberately breaking off bunches of leaves and placing them in their little mouths with a quick delicate flick of a trunk. His favorite of all the animals (until later, when he met his first gorilla), he never tired of observing their calm, dignified habits and their grand manner, or of admiring their incredible intelligence.

Happily he followed the herd over mile after mile

of grassland where they grazed their way along beneath the acacia trees.

Presently the flat landscape became rolling hills. The air turned fresh. He was in high country now, rugged and mountainous. It all looked so like the Highlands of Kenya that he was moved close to tears of homesickness.

Then late in the afternoon there rose to the right side of his path the high black foothills of a mighty mountain range. Straight up from the floor of the Western Rift Valley soared the legendary Mountains of the Moon, the Ruwenzori Range, six ice-coated peaks that the natives call *ruenjura*—the rain-makers. But although he knew the mountains were there beside him, a huge massif towering seventeen thousand feet, they were invisible that day as they are almost every day of the year, hidden in the mists and clouds that swirl about them. Many months later Jeremy would have the rare experience of viewing the Mountains of the Moon from his eagle's nest perch high atop one of the Virunga Volcanoes. But on this day the mysterious Congo beckoned him.

"Parc Albert," read the sign. It was the first indication that he had crossed the border between British and Belgian territory, having wandered across it as freely as the herds of elephant that graze from one national park to another with fine disregard for international borders. If animals don't need visas, then people shouldn't either, decided Jeremy.

His first view of the Belgian Congo was a breathtaking scene bathed in the golden light of a setting sun. Down in the valley was a sandbar island where the Semliki River drains out of Lake Edward to begin twisting northward on its way to Lake Albert. And here he came upon the meeting place of flocks of gorgeous waterfowl as they massed each dusk, presenting a great theatrical display of exotic plumage. Cormorants, pelicans, storks, herons, egrets, ibises, and all sorts of water birds mingled here, looking immensely elegant as they went about their elaborate ceremonies of courting, preening, feeding.

As he edged closer to the birds he was struck by their indifference to his presence; they were as tame as if there had never been a time when men hunted them for their plumage—hunted them almost to extinction.

He recalled, then, the way the animals in the park had ignored the human intruder with his lethal weapons; mild curiosity was the strongest reaction to his presence in these parks.

This made him wonder: It didn't seem natural, or rather it seemed too natural, the way it must have been before the Europeans came to Africa and started blowing the heads off every animal in sight. Now in all the game reserves and national parks there were these poor dumb creatures going calmly about their business as though it were going to last forever—as if those people in the overcrowded villages weren't going to need all this land, this two-million-acre zoo that was Albert National Park and all the reserves in Uganda and

Kenya and Tanganyika.

"What will become of the animals?" he asked aloud. "Where will the elephants go?" But of course he knew. And inside him welled up the first sympathy he had ever felt for Africa's wild animals.

There are some people who always have to see what is on the other side of the mountain, and Jeremy Jenkins was now one of them. Exhilarated by the familiar-looking landscape—a rift valley much like the one he had left except for the lakes that line it—and buoyed up by the crisp, cold air of the mountains on the far side of the valley, he was not prepared for the letdown at Beni.

Beni was a small trading town at a crossroads, both of which headed roughly north-south but not west. The only reason for its existence here, as far as he could determine, was that there was no place to go—not westward, anyway. For at the very edges of the roads began the silent emptiness of a dripping tropical rain forest: the Ituri, fifty thousand square miles of it. And the Ituri is only one section of the enormous forest belt that stretches as far westward as a person's mind can imagine. Starting at the foot of the Mountains of the Moon and continuing all the way to the Atlantic Ocean there is nothing except more of the same dark, dense, green rain forest flowing across the floor of the Congo Basin.

The end of the trail, he decided, for there could be no thought of venturing into that dripping darkness. No one ever does. Henry Stanley went into the Ituri three times before he found the source of the Congo River, but he lost hundreds of porters through fever, starvation, drowning, murder, opium, and God knows what else.

One of the Greek shopkeepers in Beni said this about the Ituri: "The forest? Only animals live there—animals and BaMbuti Pygmies who are like animals the way they scurry about in there."

At that moment, if anyone had told Jeremy that he was going into that threatening darkness, and going into it unarmed, he would have said they were balmy. But that was because when he first arrived at the edge of it and peered into its wet gloom, he was still an outsider. He was, like most people, a dweller in wide open spaces where there is sunlight and warmth and a vast, visible sky. Even in this hot, dry, ugly little trading town on the wrong side of the mountains, one was still conscious of a high, ever-changing African sky. There is no sky in the greenhouse that is a tropical rain forest, where gigantic trees never cease to drip water from their high leaves, and where a dense green roof keeps even a glimmer of sunlight from reaching the ground.

The way it happened is that he was spending the night as a guest of the BaBira, one of the Bantu-speaking tribes, who are forest cultivators, having cut an unsightly bald gash out of the surrounding forest in order to make plantations. The night was unbearably hot and humid, and Jeremy, lying on a sleeping mat on the earthen floor of an airless hut, sweltered as he listened to the soft calling voices of the restless Negroes who seemed never to settle down to sleep.

From outside the hut came the strange, sinister sounds of the African night; inside was the whine of mosquitoes. He was being bitten repeatedly by attacking mosquitoes and termites, and was worrying that some of the mosquitoes carried malaria, because many of the villagers were afflicted by it. Others had leprosy, or the effects of polio. The water was filthy, causing him to worry about typhoid, then about cholera, then about the tse-tse fly that carries sleeping sickness. The Congo, the heart of Stanley's Dark Continent, has ways of repelling white people.

The village was an ugly clearing of trodden, choking dust swarming with flies that covered the children's faces and the food and the contaminated water. He could hardly wait for morning when it would be light enough to leave. As soon as the cock crows, he decided, and the village women emerge from their huts to start work in the fields. He would not even wait for the meal of cold boiled millet or whatever.

But in the morning his plans were changed. And in a deep and subtle way his life was changed, too.

As he emerged from the hut at the crack of dawn he wondered that not even a shade tree was allowed to grow near the plantations. "It is from the plantations that food comes," explained one of the villagers, "not from the forest. If we do not keep back the forest it will grow over us."

That brooding wood did indeed seem to be waiting

its chance to move forward and envelope the clearing and the crude huts: waiting until the soil was exhausted and the people moved to another site, waiting to take back what was its own.

This Bira village, like so many Central African villages, was nothing more than two facing rows of mud huts and a *baraza:* a meeting place constructed of a roof supported by poles but no walls. The ground around the *baraza,* like the ground all around the village, was nothing but dry, scuffed dust.

Then Jeremy saw him. There in the *baraza* stood what he called his "first Pygmy." No more than four feet high, with skin color of yellow-red-brown, he had short legs, a protruding belly, and a body that was wiry, well-knit, and muscular, if rather swaybacked. Like a coiled spring he was, his wide-apart eyes darting this way and that and repeatedly coming to rest on Jeremy, but without any show of surprise. He carried a spear a foot taller than himself.

Onto the dust the little man threw the carcass of an animal which interested Jeremy almost as much as did the Pygmy, for it was one of those okapis he had heard about—a local forest animal that is striped vertically like a bongo. Yet an okapi is a giraffe while a bongo is an antelope. And the Pygmy was clearly offering the dead animal to the village chief, a tall Negro.

Jeremy edged closer to the *baraza,* whereupon the Pygmy turned upon him a frank and lively glance.

"I am Tefu. I am a Pygmy," he said in English.

Astonished, Jeremy blurted out: "Where did you learn English?"

"From the tourists." He grinned with a wide pixie mouth. "They drive into Beni and blow their horns. Some of us come running out of the forest. They give us cigarettes and money. They take pictures. They say, 'Aren't they ugly? They smell bad.' " He made a face in imitation. "We use the money to buy palm wine. I know French, too."

One could not help being captivated by the man's cheerful candor. Nor could one pack up and leave when Tefu said, "I have walked many hours through the forest to look upon the small English whose presence here was reported throughout the forest." So the three of them—the tall black chief, the short brown Pygmy, and the "small English"—sat on the floor of the *baraza* and passed around a gourd of palm wine while an audience of villagers stared at them.

The chief explained to Jeremy that each village in this area has its own Pygmies and that the Negroes are their masters. He used the word *bakpara,* which means something like "owners" or "dominators of." He further stated that the BaMbuti (which means "of the Mbuti tribe") are like animals, having no culture of their own nor any religion either; that they gratefully accept the authority of the Negoes in all matters of importance: birth, burial, initiation, and so forth.

"Nonsense," retorted Jeremy. "Everyone knows that the Negroes came to this part of Africa only lately, while Pygmies, on the other hand, have lived all through the rain forests of the Congo since long ago, and may even be the oldest people in Africa. Surely the entire Pygmy race, including these BaMbuti, have *some* kind of religion: doesn't everybody? Why do you Negroes make laborers out of these Pygmies?"

"They don't mind," answered the chief, while Tefu nodded agreement.

As the gourd of bitter-tasting brew went the rounds, the chief and Tefu began discussing the coming *nkumbi,* which was held in this village every three years. *Nkumbi* was the traditional festival in which all the boys between the ages of nine and twelve were circumcised and then kept for three months in initiation camps where they were subjected to harsh treatment and taught the secrets of the tribe. The boys emerged from all this with the status of men.

Jeremy yawned with boredom and drowsiness. Hardly anything new about that. Having lived among various African tribes all his life, he was certainly familiar with the tribal ritual of initiation, instruction, circumcision: puberty rites for African boys who have come of age. He had even been allowed to witness some of the Kikuyu rites of passage.

But there was something odd going on here. Was he to understand from the talk that these BaMbuti Pygmies send their own sons out of the forest and into the villages to be initiated along with the BaBira boys of the same age? And instructed by the elders of the Bira tribe instead of by their own tribesmen?

Addressing Tefu, he asked, "Aren't the BaMbuti hunters?"

"The greatest hunters in the world," answered Tefu, banging a fist on his chest.

"Then why do you permit your sons to be initiated into a village culture where people do not hunt but instead plant vegetables?"

"You are smart, small English; you have guessed that when a BaMbuti boy is old enough his true initiation comes on the day he kills his first real game—a buffalo, an antelope, an okapi: something big. I myself killed an elephant, but few possess such courage as I."

"Bully for you," acknowledged Jeremy, truly impressed. "But, Tefu, why would the boys of a hunting tribe need initiation into a village tribe?"

"Ask him," replied Tefu, indicating the chief.

The chief took another swallow of palm wine before answering. "Because the BaMbuti are in need of guidance in matters of witchcraft and sorcery. We BaBira have knowledge of such things and they do not."

"What a lot of rot!" An explosion was building up in Jeremy's head. He scrambled to his feet, buckled once, and staggered away from the *baraza*. "Primitive savage claptrap," he muttered as he stumbled across the clearing to his hut. Outside the hut he was sick. *Sick of people, that's what I am. Savages! Barbarians!*

He was thinking of the Kikuyu tribe and of their ignorant superstitious fear of witchcraft and sorcery and black magic and evil spirits and all the rest of that rubbish. And he was convinced that if the Kikuyu had managed to rid themselves of their superstitious awe of magic, all that voodoo could not have been used by the Kikuyus' more educated leaders to turn their fellow tribesmen into cutthroats—used to make them drink oath, kill their bwanas, burn the farms, terrorize the Highlands and drive the colonists out of Kenya.

He could feel the strokes of his blood pounding in his ears, and he knew if he stayed in this wretched village with its stagnant superstitious people he would let loose all his pent-up anger. So he began to gather up his gear, now acutely aware that he had a long trek ahead of him before he would be able to breathe fresh mountain air again and drink fresh mountain water in a world cleansed by cold and wind. There was a part of Uganda he had always wanted to see because it was called "the Switzerland of Africa." A resort region of clear lakes and wooded hills, it thrust like an arrowhead between the Congo and Ruanda: a tiny kingdom that was Belgian Trust territory.

But there was some disturbance going on in the *baraza*. The chief and Tefu were looking at him and arguing—at least they were gesturing and talking excitedly. What now? Another delay?

The chief approached. Jeremy stiffened and waited. The chief addressed him in Swahili:

"Have you been initiated?"

Jeremy gaped, feeling none too bright at this point.

"Initiated into what, for God's sake?"

"Have you been circumcised?"

"That is none of your business."

"Do not think *I* ask; Tefu asks."

Indeed, there was Tefu smiling and waving from the *baraza*.

The chief said, "Unless one is initiated one is a *miki* —a child—no matter if he be a grown man or old."

"What's that to do with me?"

"Tefu asks because he wants to take you home with him, into the forest. It is for that reason he came . . . and brought the okapi meat. He may take it back if you do not go."

"Me? Why me?"

The chief shrugged. "Maybe because you are short, like him. Maybe because you are white. Maybe because all BaMbuti are crazy." He laughed a loud offensive laugh.

"Jolly good of Tefu," said Jeremy in his most formal manner. "I suppose I'm honored, but you see I have to . . ." He broke off, unable to think of a suitable excuse. Nor did he want to offend that bright little gnome of a man who was waving and grinning at him from his place on the *baraza* steps. Besides, he felt his head spinning with the heat and the glare of the sun on the dry scuffed dust—and perhaps with a little too much palm wine.

Jeremy leaned forward confidentially and whispered in a dramatic tone: "Are they cannibals?"

Again the big voice boomed with coarse laughter. "The only cannibals around here are BaNgwana, a tribe of witches that make strong black magic and cast strong evil spells. But we do not mix with them." The chief spat elaborately three times on the dust. "They are Islamic. They helped the slavers."

He went on: "There is no doubt that these BaMbuti are more trouble than they are worth: lazy, thieving, good for nothing, always disappearing into their forest when there is work to be done; always changing the place of their camps to avoid being found when we send for them. They are mischievous like children, but, like children, harmless. Besides, they bring us meat from the forest. But they are crazy. They prove this by singing songs to the forest as if the forest has ears like a man." He grinned with superiority.

"What is it like in the forest?" Jeremy asked him, regarding the wall of trees with new curiosity.

The grin was erased suddenly. The chief's eyes widened and rolled toward that impenetrable darkness that bordered the fields.

"We never go far into the forest; only enough for cutting wood." He fingered the charm he wore about his neck, lowered his voice, and said, "Evil spirits live in there. It is a place of sorcery, not fit to be lived in except by animals. Nor do we walk through it even to visit our kin in the near village. In there dwells a presence which casts spells on us, causing us to die, or to be possessed. People have disappeared in its depths."

Jeremy strained his gaze toward the trees, trying to imagine that dense primeval forest stretching silent and aloof, wet and dark with mystery, its ages-old trees brooding over an eternal gloom. Scary in a way. And yet there was something fascinating about its very mystery, its very remoteness, which seemed to be drawing him physically toward it in a way that his addled brain did not even try to analyze. It was as if—as if that vast sea of trees was waiting to embrace him, to shelter him from the outside world—from dusty, parched, listless villages of stagnation and boredom. The wood was inviting him to cool his hot anger in its soothing, damp shade.

To his wavering vision the trees seemed to sway. They were beckoning him to come, to be taken into the heart of the forest. And like a sleepwalker Jeremy opened his arms to the trees, and he walked toward them so that he and the trees might possess each other.

Several hours later, jogging behind Tefu in that green underwater world, he understood the reason the magic of the forest called to him. During the past few weeks he had been fleeing from something—something he was not yet ready to think about, for to think about it would cause pain. He had a longing for privacy and seclusion. Like a wounded animal, he had an instinct to hide, and in the same sort of place a wounded animal seeks out: a dark place, restful and quiet.

The rain forest was like an ocean in that the deeper they went into it, the darker it became.

At the first stream they came to Tefu waded in and washed himself, explaining that he cleansed himself of the dirty village so that he might re-enter the sacred place of the forest in purity. And while Jeremy was doing likewise he was struck with wonder at how quickly he, an outsider, adapted to the cool, damp shade. He did not feel at all uneasy or hemmed in because, even though the towering trees met so close overhead that they shut out the sun, the floor was spacious and clear of growth. Nor did he feel overpowered by the remoteness of this place from the outside world, even though he knew that to the south much of the Ituri is unexplored.

On the contrary, the deeper they went into the gloom the freer he felt. It was as if he had reached a haven where he could expand and be his real self. His Pygmy guide, too, dropped the constraints of the village where he was too shy to speak for himself. Also he dropped that false mask of servility he presented in front of the village chief. This he explained by saying, "Only in the forest am I free."

In the months to come—those months of joyous existence on the forested slopes of the volcanoes—Jeremy was to recall those words of Tefu's and to know the experience of finding an almost holy release in a cathedral of smooth, branchless, soaring tree trunks beneath towering arches of leaves.

Then, farther on, Jeremy's happiness was shattered by an unfortunate accident. At least it seemed unfortunate at the time. He lost his guns, both of them. The ammunition box too. It happened when they were crossing the Ituri River, which Tefu said was higher than usual because of the torrential rains which overloaded the streams that flow from a great mountain range to the east—the ones called Mountains of the Moon.

Tefu was in water up to his eyes and having a hard enough time fording the broad Ituri, which seemed determined to sweep them with it all the way to the Aruwimi River and thence to the mighty Congo for which it was bound. But the Pygmy was accustomed to crossing water because the Ituri Forest is laced with many tributaries, all of them feeding the same thirsty Congo. Besides, Tefu had the advantage of weighing almost nothing and of being nearly naked. He wore only a loincloth made of hammered bark: a long, narrow strip tucked between his legs and into his belt. Also he was barefoot.

Jeremy, an awkward outsider from country high and dry, was clumsily overdressed in jacket and leather boots as well as being loaded down with heavy artillery. When he felt his foot slip on a submerged rock and found himself clutching at nothing but water on his way downstream, he knew he would have to jettison the guns. The only thought that crossed his mind was that he had carried these guns all this way without once firing them, and now that he was within inches of plentiful and unprotected game, the blasted things were trying to drown him.

How would he get along without his guns? It was no consolation when Tefu reminded him that a gunshot in the forest would scare more game than it would kill; he knew that. Nor did it help for Tefu to offer the gift of his own bow and spear. How could any Pygmy understand that a white man feels vulnerable without his guns?

In a few hours he would be surprised to find himself feeling curiously lightened, relieved not only physically but also mentally by the loss of those burdensome reminders of his past life. But now, sprawled on the ground with his guide while the wet clothes were spread to dry, he felt only desolation.

Tefu, in his own forest, assumed a new dignity and showed an unsuspected sensitivity. This little man, so full of native wisdom, succeeded in diverting Jeremy's thoughts and dispelling his despair with tales about himself and his family, which included more kin than most people are able to keep track of. Tefu was animated and chattering, boasting of his prowess as a hunter of elephant, or *mbongu*. Jeremy let himself be entertained.

When Tefu spoke of the villagers he sneered. "The *batu banji* are a race of tall, clumsy individuals unable to run as one must run through the forest: swiftly and silently like a shadow. Like elephants they scare the game; they trip, and bang their heads." He demonstrated this so comically that Jeremy hurt from laughter.

"We Mbuti make use of the villagers, stealing from them at night as the baboons do—always the ripest fruit—and we trade our meat for their iron which we need for spear blades. The *batu banji* say we are lazy

—will not pick their cotton or plant their beans. But we cannot, because away from our forest we die—yes, die of sunstroke." He collapsed in mock faint.

"And if we work on their *tikos* who will hunt with bow and poisoned arrow? Or *ekonga?*" He patted his long spear. "Among Mbuti laziness is a crime; it is the only crime we BaMbuti have. In our tribe is a saying: 'The only hungry Mbuti is a lazy Mbuti.' None of us need be hungry because the *ndura*"—he waved an arm at the wood—"provides all: meat, mushrooms, nuts, sweet roots, berries. For shelter it provides mongongo leaves for building huts to keep off the rain.

"You will like the forest, small English," he said with a broad grin. "Do not be sad about your guns; you are not like the others." His eyes were twinkling with secret knowledge.

Just what the Pygmy meant by that was not clear. But now Jeremy felt secure enough with his host to inquire about the religion of the BaMbuti. Upon Tefu's face spread an expression of solemnity, of reverence, of devout faith without awe, without trace of fear. His eyes shone bright with ecstatic joy as he said:

"The Spirit of the Forest is our mother and our father. Thus we reverence it. The *ndura* gives us not only food and shelter and warmth of fire, but love, and life: like a parent. For we are *bamiki ba ndura*—children of the forest."

"Oh, how beautiful!" exclaimed his listener. "So much better than the Christian God who is always judging and punishing and causing His children to be afraid of doing something wrong. He, too, is a father; but a stern one, to be feared."

"I am sorry," said Tefu simply.

Then he went on to describe for Jeremy a life of singing and dancing. "Sometimes things go wrong in the forest. To awaken the Spirit of the Forest so it will hear of our troubles, every Pygmy in the camp sings. We sing all through the night and the next night. We hunters dance by the light of the fire."

Here Tefu demonstrated. In a trance-like state, eyes open and bright with worship, he danced: danced with the trees, with the forest itself; whirling and skipping, leaping and twisting; his little arms outstretched, raised upward; his lithe body abandoned in a dance of devotion, of exaltation, of gratitude and praise for the forest that provides life. It was a dance of supreme joy, a dance of love.

Jeremy was deeply moved, and impressed. It's almost like a religious service, he thought, except that there's no church, and he's alone, and sort of free. It's almost like our communion. Gosh! It *is* communion.

After that they continued on their way through the forest at a fast jog, the somber shadows amid the dim green filtered light all but concealing the little brown figure up ahead, which seemed to appear and disappear as if it were an illusion made by a magician. Twice Jeremy passed right by his guide without seeing him, so perfectly did the body of the Pygmy blend with the foliage. And if it had not been for intermittent glimpses of a woolly globular head bobbing ahead of him, Jeremy would have thought himself skimming across the open forest floor in a dream.

Indeed, in the months to come, and as that brief visit to the Ituri Forest receded in Jeremy's memory, he wondered now and again if it had been real—if he had actually met that band of Pygmies and lived among them; if he had come to know Tefu's numerous kinsmen; if the women had fashioned for him, Jeremy Jenkins, his own small hut made of mongongo leaves; if he had really helped brown Pygmy boys to hold the net of woven vines into which the women and children drove an antelope, and joined those boys in catching the animal with their bare hands when it escaped the net. Had it happened?

Often he asked himself this question during the solitary times that came later, when he was leading his peculiar woodland existence on the volcanoes.

"Of course it happened," he told himself. If he had not done those things then how would he, a kid from the Highlands, know how to survive in a forest wilderness? How would he know how to capture game with his bare hands? How would he know where to look for wild fruits he might have passed by? Where to find the sweeter-tasting roots? Under what kind of leaves one searches for the newly sprouted mushrooms? Who but the Pygmies would have taught him never to own more possessions than he could carry on his back, never to make a permanent camp? And above all, who but those people who sang the praises of the forest could have taught him that the forest will provide for anyone who allows himself to come under its spell and gives it his trust?

When the day finally came that Tefu returned his guest to the outside world at the edge of the road in Beni, he again made the observation:

"You, small English, are not like the others. For you the gun is not necessary."

And Tefu made a prediction:

"Someday you will become like me, *miki nde ndura*." It meant "son of the forest."

Chapter Six

Uhuru

Wanderlust. It does strange things to people. Before he had the experience of traversing Uganda, skirting the Mountains of the Moon, and visiting a rain forest, Jeremy had never in his life been more than fifty miles from the Highlands of Kenya. Now he was setting out to see Africa, carrying with him nothing more than a knife, a compass, and a few firm convictions—all, at one time or another, given him by his father.

He was also well supplied with foodstuffs. His Pygmy host, Tefu, had stuffed the knapsack with mushrooms, dried monkey meat, dried okapi meat, and certain unidentified edibles that looked suspiciously like termites.

After Tefu returned him to the crossroads at Beni, the Greek shopkeeper there arranged transportation south for him in a truck bound for Ruanda.

Jeremy expected their route would be through that very part of Uganda he had always wanted to see. It is only one day's drive from Beni, and besides it is the shortest route to Ruanda. But things did not turn out as expected.

The truck was one left over from the war. The driver was a chocolate-brown man about the same size as Jeremy himself: a Batwa Pygmy who spoke English like a Frenchman and who drove with speed and skill.

The man introduced himself by saying, "We Batwa are a hunting tribe like your friends the BaMbuti who occupy the Ituri Forest. Batwa territory is *there*." He waved to indicate the Rift Mountains that march along the western edge of the Rift Valley. But anyone could see just by looking that many of the trees had been cut down to make clearings for little plots of vegetables and clusters of thatched huts.

"Not much game there, I'll warrant," remarked Jeremy.

The Batwa explained. "Some of my tribe are still hunters, carrying two spears in one hand and a machete in the other. But, I regret to say, others are beggars. This is because the local Bantus have taken much of our forest for their own use, which is to plant fields. I myself am neither hunter nor beggar. I walked every day to the mission school to learn the lessons and the foreigner's language. When came *la guerre* I learned how to drive a *sortie,* or what you English call a lorry."

Their southward route, it soon became apparent, was to be up, down, and around the Rift Mountains. The long way around. Jeremy was disappointed, but only momentarily.

"To avoid the passing of two customs posts: one upon entering Uganda and the other upon leaving," explained the driver. "We keep to this highway on the Congo side of the valley; then cut across Parc Albert to Lac Kivu, and *voilà!* Ruanda—Belgian territory—without the need to answer questions or submit to inspection."

"I hadn't thought of that," said Jeremy.

To himself he said, "Stupid! When you're a fugitive you're supposed to keep things like that in mind. I'd need a passport to get through the other way. And wouldn't I look silly being hauled off this lorry by the British officials in Uganda, taken into whatever they call it—protective custody—and sent back? That was a narrow escape, and not by half. About this Batwa, though, I wonder what he has in the back of this truck that he doesn't want inspected?"

At this point the driver made a surprisingly abrupt announcement:

"Independence is coming to the Congo," he declared. "In a few years there will be no Belgians in the Congo."

"Why not? I mean where will they be?" He added, "sir."

"Dead, *mon ami.* Or fled. All foreigners: dead or fled."

Jeremy gasped. Having little knowledge of the politics of other countries, he assumed that only where Europeans had farms, as in Kenya, was there reason for a native uprising. The Congo seemed as peaceful as Uganda, for here, also, it was the natives who were the landowners. And what could cause a revolt except a land dispute? Surely this Batwa was mistaken.

"All foreigners?" he asked.

"Oui."

"Father said that he and I are as African as the baobab tree, and every bit as impossible to uproot from the land. I would not be considered a foreigner, would I?"

The driver, who was sitting on a cushion so he could see over the steering wheel, glanced down at his passenger's hands. *"Oui."*

That simple "Yes" demolished Jeremy's hopes of finding refuge here in the Congo.

His mind dizzy with confusion, uncertainty, apprehension, he asked, "Sir, where in Africa could a white person like me be safe? I mean for a long time, or until this trouble is over?"

"Everywhere it will be the same," replied the man matter-of-factly. *"Uhuru.* Freedom. Self-government."

"I don't understand."

"Few do, *mon ami,* few do. But they will understand when two hundred million Africans rise up with a single cry: *'Uhuru'!* It is the Swahili word for 'Freedom'! Freedom from white rule."

"But sir, how will the Africans manage without the Europeans to take care of things for them?"

The driver was silent for several minutes. At length he spoke, slowly, as if translating his thoughts into careful English.

"You see now black Africa, innocent like a young child who is cared for by its father—but also dominated by him. Arrives then the time for black Africa to come of age and be no longer so innocent. Compare this to the coming-of-age of one African child. There are rites of passage, yes? And they include pain, do they not? Just so, the rites of passage for emerging

Africa will include much pain for its people. And bloodshed—years of savage bloodshed."

"I hope it won't be like Kenya," said Jeremy with a tremor in his voice. And there flashed through his squeezed-shut eyes the vision of cattle with their throats cut, cows with their udders slashed off, lowing and writhing in agony . . . black smoke rising from acres of farmland . . . a corpse with blood oozing out from the place where the head should be. . . .

He saw himself. He was running, running all over the continent from one country to another with no place to stop and rest. Or else hiding. Running and hiding from fanatical blacks who didn't even know *why* they were out to kill him, only that an order had been given and they had to obey their king: the *kabaka* or the *mwami* or the *ganwa* or the tribal chief or whoever their people had been trained for thousands of years to obey. And he thought of his guns lying at the bottom of the Ituri River.

"You say that *everywhere* it will be the same?" he asked, "the whole continent?"

"C'est inevitable," the driver replied firmly.

Jeremy turned his face to the window as if to seek the answer there, and he peered intently at the faces of the Negroes who were walking along the sides of the highway or making repairs on the road.

The women had babies riding in slings on their backs or children running along beside them, or both. They carried bundles on their heads, or water jugs, which gave to their stride grace and dignity. The women smiled broadly at his straining face, and the children waved greetings. The men stopped their desultory picking at the road to grin and salute, the way the Belgians had taught the natives to salute all white people. None of these Africans looked like angry rebels who wanted to get rid of the white foreigner so they could own his imported motorcar and dress in his imported business suit. They seemed content with the male costume that is seen all over: army surplus clothing left over from the war, the favorite being heavy army overcoats too big for them. And the women wore their brightly colored prints with a kind of style. Jeremy wondered if these people knew about *Uhuru.*

But then an oncoming car, a Ford with a Congo license plate, slowed as it drew near. The two Africans in the car exchanged with the truck driver a signal also left over from the war. It was two fingers held up in a V for Victory sign. This little conspiracy gave Jeremy a vague feeling of menace, causing him to shiver involuntarily, which, in turn, caused him to remark hastily that it turns cold up here in the mountains.

The Batwa agreed, lit a cigarette made of loose tobacco rolled in newspaper, then proceeded to point out every structure in the hills that was a Christian mission.

"They, too, will have to go," he said. "Both the *Wa Franza* (French Catholics) and the *Wa Ingrezi* (English Protestants)."

Then with unexpected passion he shot out the words: "White Christians! They severed the hands of Congolese. Surprised, are you not?"

Jeremy was horrified.

"*Mais oui.* Under Leopold Two of Belgium, who took for his personal self the rubber and the ivory from the Congo. But, *mon Dieu,* how he obtained it! Baskets full of human hands, chopped off if a worker was too slow. Also, for each cartridge issued to a Belgian soldier there was obliged to be brought in a part of a human body. *Oui.* To prove there was no waste. Belgians are frugal people. Ha ha."

Silence in the truck as Jeremy tried to put this together with what Father always said.

When speaking of the Mau Mau and their own hideous kind of atrocity, Father always said, "Those people are heathens, not guided by the ways of the Lord. Christians do not do such things." He said the same thing about the Arab slavers who took Negroes out of Africa in chains. He said, "Those people are Moslems; they don't know any better." And about any Africans who had not yet been converted to Christianity, Father always said, "Those people are pagans, unbelievers; it is the duty of us Christians to show them the light."

"But that's all over with now, isn't it? The colonists are kind to their workers now, aren't they? Father always was." Jeremy waited anxiously for the answer.

"Ha!" exclaimed the Batwa. "If you think it is kind

to force Negroes into the coffee plantations at gun-point. This is done by the Belgian overseers."

Jeremy was biting his fingernails the way he used to do at home. The driver glanced over at him and changed the subject to one he doubtless thought would be interesting to a young boy.

"See down there?" He pointed westward to where the mountains dropped down to the Congo Basin. There was nothing to see, really, except the tops of trees; all the way to the horizon stretched a lumpy green carpet. "There is the Maniema Forest where live tribes of cannibals. They trade in human flesh, buying, selling, eating it. One tribe will capture people of another tribe then sell them, for use like your *boeuf*—or beef. Perhaps they cook it first; perhaps not. I would not wish to find out. Everyone stays away from that forest even as did your great Livingstone and your Stanley. Even the Arab slaving gangs feared to go there."

Jeremy strained his gaze downward, as if it could penetrate the sea of foliage. But the forest remained solid, motionless, heavy-looking; and it kept its awful secrets in the dark.

Obviously pleased with the impression he was making on his listener, the driver added, "*Mais, oui;* why do you think no white man set eyes upon these mountains nor upon Lac Edward or Lac Kivu until only sixty years ago?"

"I never thought about it."

"*Oui,* that is why. And now, *voilà!* we have this highway engineered well by the Belgians, and this *sortie* that goes so fast, and petrol, and," he laughed, "an educated Pygmy for a driver. Were it not for the white foreigners this Batwa would be begging, or starving."

"But I thought you Africans didn't like the colonists being in your country? You said the Congolese are going to chuck the Belgians out of the Congo."

"That is correct. Before five years. Freedom. *Uhuru.*" Jeremy felt stunned by what seemed a contradiction. But his attention was taken by new scenery.

In the distance was a lake glittering in the afternoon sun. As it came closer he saw that gathered around the lake were Europeans sunning themselves amid bright beach umbrellas. All around the shores were modern hotels, and on the lake, motorboats and sailboats.

"We are coming into Goma," the driver announced. "Only two kilometers beyond Goma is the Ruanda border. There I deliver my cargo."

Attempting an offhand attitude, Jeremy asked, "What *is* our cargo?"

"Machine guns. Rifles. Ammunition." The truck slowed for the sharp left-hand turn, which brought the lake straight ahead.

"You see, *mon ami,* although I, a Batwa, am no lover of Bantu Negroes—and care nothing for those Bantus of the Bahutu tribe in Ruanda—I like even less the Watusi. I dislike *all* oppressors, whatever their color. And those Tutsi hold the Hutu like slaves. For thousands of years, the *mwami* of Ruanda is a Tutsi; those warriors, good for nothing but playing games and dancing, are the ruling class, the overlords, like your feudal barons."

"And so you supply guns to your old enemies, a tribe of Bantu Negroes?"

"We not-so-tall people have to stick together, *n'est-ce pas?*" The Pygmy poked him and laughed.

He's trying to make a joke of it so I'll only half believe him about the guns, said Jeremy to himself. Still, people say the Watusi conquered the Bahutu by intimidating them with their sheer height, for Bahutu are short people and Watusi are supposed to be seven feet tall.

"There are some Tutsi now, playing football." The driver pointed to a group of boys dressed in striped jerseys and white shorts, kicking a round ball.

Now here was something Jeremy understood. He played football, or soccer, in school and in the Kikuyu compound.

"Stop! I'll get out here."

Instantly he was a schoolboy again: lighthearted, carefree, unconcerned with the troubles of the world. He felt almost *right* again, like a former self half remembered, a former friend half recognized. He had to explore this feeling.

"*Merci, monsieur.* And good luck to you on your errand."

"*Attention.*" The driver held his arm. "You must not stay in this place for long. These firearms I transport are meant to be used. The oppressed shall rise up against the oppressor. Hutu against Tutsi. Congolese against Belgian. Black against white. I tell you this, *mon ami,* so that you will not be overtaken by the revolution. I tell you this because I have the notion that you—being *Ingrezi* from Kenya—have suffered already from the great cause." With a *"Vive l'Indepen-dence!"* he saluted. *"Au revoir, mon ami."* The gears of the truck clashed.

As Jeremy watched the truck disappear down the road he was struck by the fact that he did not know the man's name, nor did the man know his. Just as well.

He watched the Watusis' game until dark. Then, eagerly, he set out to absorb all of Goma's sights. How long it had been since he had seen a European town! Not since Nairobi. This one was different. Very small; and the language that flowed through its streets was French.

He gave himself over to the sensation of experiencing this gay town after being so long away from civilization: of looking in shop windows at imported things from Paris and Brussels; of walking past tidy pastel-colored villas; and then, of swimming off a white sand beach in bright moonlight.

The native sector was a shantytown. Here, the same as in the farming villages, the Negroes were mighty drinkers of banana beer. But these people, rather than being listless and stupefied, roared along the streets or danced with wild abandon.

Caught up in the free spirit of these Central Africans, he dared to strike up an acquaintance with an official-looking African who was sitting in a sidewalk café, sucking banana beer from a gourd with a long spout. The man wore a uniform of khaki shirt and shorts and a dark green fez upon which was a gold insignia. But his feet were bare, and his teeth were filed into points like a cannibal's.

Now, if ever an encounter was preordained, that one was. Often, while Jeremy was living on the volcanoes, his thoughts went back to that lucky chance meeting in Goma. For the filed-toothed African was one of the guards assigned to Albert Park. His job, as he explained in Swahili, was to march in military formation at park headquarters in Rumangabo. "For that we carry spears," he said proudly.

"Is that all you do?" asked his listener.

"Sometimes I hire my services to visitors as a guide in the park. Then, too, there is the unending task of chasing the Watusi and their flea-bitten cattle out of the park where they bring them to graze, and sometimes shooting a few of their cows. Also I am supposed to look out for poachers in the park, and . . . oh, yes: guard the gorillas."

"Gorillas? In the park? I always thought gorillas lived in the jungle."

"Up there." The African waved his arm toward the north, indicating a group of volcanic mountains that looked dark and forbidding.

Later that night Jeremy was sprawled on the sandy

beach, but without thought of sleeping. After a day packed with new impressions his mind was racing. Especially keen was that shock he had felt, and was still feeling, at the idea of any uprising. "Gad! A native revolt! Here! Why bother to leave Kenya? May as well get killed one place as another."

He was lying on his back, gazing upward at the black shapes of the volcanoes. Those forests up there, he mused. I'll wager they're not too different from the forests on Mount Kenya or the Aberdares. Not as high as old Kerinyagga, but the same bald top, the same rain forest, the same evergreen woodland, bamboo . . . Game probably as scarce as in the Aberdares where those Mau Mau have their hideouts. *Hideout!* Something clicked.

"Wizard!" he shouted, and was shaken by such a surge of wild elation that he threw off his clothes and ran, splashing, into the silver-plated lake. Maybe the chilly water would cool his brain, because a more sensible self was saying: What an absolutely balmy idea! You've gone round the bend, my boy. Daft, that's what you are. Forget it!

He floated on his back, considering: "If it can be done why hasn't somebody done it before? Maybe someone has. Who would know? Gosh! You could live like Robinson Crusoe. Not a ruddy person up there. But hold on there. No one is allowed on the volcanoes; the guard said so.

"That guard!" he snorted. "That drunken cannibal

is afraid of those forests—you could tell. And the look on his face when he mentioned the gorillas! He's terrified of them. I'll wager he's never even seen one. How about when I asked him, 'Do you think you could show me a gorilla?' The cannibal said, 'If you call the gorilla by name you will never find it.' Then he said something more sensible:

"He said, 'If you were one of the world's greatest scientists, and if you wrote a letter to the Institute of Congo Parks in Brussels, Belgium, requesting permission to search for gorilla in the Bufumbiro Mountains; and if my commandant wrote a letter, too, you might get a pass good for ten days—taking me along, of course, as guide. But you would be wasting your time because you would not see a gorilla.' When I asked him 'Why not?' he said, 'There is no use in searching for those gorillas. They do not exist except in imagination.' "

Whether the gorillas existed or not didn't matter: he was going. His heart pounded with the certainty of it. It was fate; fate meant him to go. Clearly that was the reason he had been put down in this spot.

There was no point in sleeping. Even before first light he was starting up the nearest slope past little native settlements, picking and eating the wild strawberries and raspberries which grew along the way.

Gradual and easy at first, the slope became steep. The woods got thicker, then stopped to give way to bamboo. His breath was coming shallow and fast. The sun became hot. He sweated, slapped at mosquitoes, reminding himself that the pesky things breed like mad in the stagnant puddles around the bamboo roots. The black ground was so slimy with leaf mold that his boots slipped on it. So he cut a bamboo pole and sharpened one end. It was both his staff and his spear. "Just in case anything sinister comes along," he said.

How wild and quiet it was, with an unearthly silence that had nothing whatsoever to do with the villages down below. Nothing to do with Jeremy Jenkins, either. The bamboo forest—damp and dense and dim —seemed hostile to humans. There was nothing in that tangled place that knew him; there were only creatures with paws. "Why did I come?" he wondered. "This is not at all like being in the Aberdares. These criss-crossed trails all look alike when you're alone.

"Well, my lad, that's what you wanted: to be alone. But not this sort of alone," he countered. "In the Queen Elizabeth Park there was all that sky showing, and the animals standing around. And in the Ituri Forest you can at least see ahead of you, see what's coming." The greenish light—what there was of it— started to fade. Night. Those creatures with paws have eyes made for seeing in the blackness that was soon to fall like an iron curtain.

The fog came in. It was then that his stomach started to burn like fury, and he recalled those peas he had eaten back there in the forest. Poison! What rotten luck. He crawled toward the sound of a running stream, drank, vomited, then lay on the leaf mold, thinking: It doesn't matter; not really. Africa would have killed me one way or another. It's out to get me, that's clear enough. Just a matter of time. May as well die here from poisoning as to have my throat cut or be shot by some crazy African. . . .

Nothing personal, mind you. It's just that you happen to have a white face. You are of the tribe called "hairy ones" whose chiefs carved up Africa like some big pie, each taking a slice. You, too, will have to go —along with the missionaries and the government officials. Along with the teachers, doctors, nurses, nuns, priests; the scientists and the rich safari people and the tourists and the crews that come from Hollywood to make films. All will have to go.

C'est inevitable.

He closed his eyes and waited for the creeping death to overtake him. He was not hurting anymore. Just tired.

Then the gorillas found him, and he thought he was imagining things. By some miracle of good health he got over his sickness. By a greater miracle they got over being frightened of him. He soon got used to them, too, becoming familiar with each one of those funny-looking faces, wrinkled like a prune. "The important thing is," he said, "these gorillas tolerate me even though I don't look like them." That was what counted most.

Thus began his time on the mountain—that is, his

109

actual time. The real joy—the solid contentment of it —did not come immediately, therefore he always thought of his real time as having started some while after he arrived, when he had done with making a simpleton of himself.

When he first arrived he was still seething with rage against—well, against everybody. Then in one day all that anger just left him. And it was because of the gorillas.

At first he did not know that you have to be careful around gorillas, that you must not make a sudden gesture with your hand or a quick motion with your arm. How was he to know, he asked himself, that gorillas are as shy as antelope? Look at the size of them! They look as if they could kill you with one hand while they're eating with the other. Who would expect them to be that spooky?

Above all, though, you must never raise your voice. Gorillas cannot stand that. Loud noises send them crashing into the bushes, and for a long time afterward they are so skittish it is impossible to come near them.

Before Jeremy knew that, he went one fine day to the high place where he could look down upon the lake at Goma. Standing there, he cupped his hands around his mouth and shrilled in his high-pitched voice as loud as he could:

"Hey you down there! Listen! D'ya hear? This is Jeremy Jenkins speaking for Radio Free Me! Go ahead and kill each other if you want. I don't care anymore!"

110

Echoes bounced around hills. The wildlife fled in a rustle of leaves.

Then he gave one more furious yell. Mixing French and Swahili he shrieked, *"Vive Uhuru!"*

He never did anything like that again.

Chapter Seven

A Parting of Ways

Once Jeremy threw his lot in with that of the gorillas, he adjusted the rhythm of his days to their indolent schedule of feeding, napping, another feeding, then early to bed. And, in time, he lost all count of the weeks and the months. Life on the mountain was too good to measure out time by knotting a cord or notching a stick each time the sun rose or the moon repeated a phase. The Spirit of the Forest was kind, and time stood still.

So the days went by, not bearing labels Saturday or Sunday or Monday, not grouping themselves into weeks and months. Only days with a beginning, a middle, and an end—a sunrise and a sunset—rainy days and sunny days.

So many of these nameless days were passed on the mountain that all the years Jeremy had existed before this time seemed far away: exactly how far away had long since ceased to concern him. His animal needs were met in the abundance of a forest whose fruits remained always in season, whose roots combined with the berries to sustain his health; whose wildlife, though sparse and elusive, was enough to satisfy his desire for meat.

Above all, his abnormal need for the healing powers of solitude had been met, along with his more normal need for congenial companionship. His existence was deeply satisfying: so much so that he forgot his anger at the world outside his sanctuary, forgot even who he was and that he was a different sort of animal from his amiable companions.

Indeed, he had come to look more like a wild animal than a well-brought-up English boy. His clothes were tattered—rent with long tears—and dark and stiff with sweat. He was not dirty because dirt, he noticed, comes only with civilization. But his body was bruised, cut, and scarred from the many gouges and scratches he received from going where the gorillas go, and from his daily hunting; it was also covered with red, itchy bites and nettle welts. His hair was always in his eyes, matted with burrs, and considerably longer, so that he tied it back with a boot lace. And, although he did not know it, there was a peculiar glint, or gleam, in his eyes that had not been there before.

He had practiced, and had learned, to move through the forest like a Pygmy, invisible and inaudible, and to hold so still that his prey was not aware of his presence. He could take almost any animal he wanted, now that he had come to recognize the spoor of all the small game.

His eyes were keener than ever; his ears and his nose he used like a dog, swiveling his head and flaring his nostrils. Now that he was hunting for subsistence rather than for sport, he felt that the wilderness had claimed him as one of its own and that he had made of himself what Tefu called *"miki nde ndura"*—son of the forest.

For while the spell of the forest heightened his perception and his animal senses, at the same time it drew a veil of forgetfulness over the events of the past few years.

The ghosts still came to his platform bed in the trees, but less frequently. Only now and then did the bodies come, carrying in their arms their severed heads. Seldom did disembodied heads float before his vision, speaking their questions with soundless lips and accusing eyes. Less and less often did the empty sleeves reach, the bony fingers point, the mouths open in screams, the eyes drip from empty sockets. Although his sleep was not as sound as that of his sleeping companions, he took as little thought as they to times past.

It is true that now and again a memory would stir in his mind, but it was more often a memory that harkened back to his early childhood, when the only fears he had were imaginary ones—when his world was small, like himself, and as innocent.

Before Jeremy came to know fear of his fellow humans he had, like all children, a fear of the dark. This returned in the black forest. And try as he might to overcome it, he was forced to admit that dusk brought a heavy depression and that each dawn was a release. Many a night he awakened before the earth had rolled quite far enough eastward. Then he would lie on his bed and repeat firmly to himself something the Pygmies had taught him:

If the darkness is, *then the darkness is good.*

114

The sunny days were the ones that Jeremy liked best. The sun did not appear often, but when it did all the gorillas would immediately stop their gorging and roll over on their backs or their sides. As for himself, spread-eagled and completely naked, he would allow the equatorial sun to burn into him until the sweat ran into his eyes and down his chest. Then he would go to a stream and splash and wallow like a hippopotamus. This always upset the gorillas because they hated to get even their feet wet.

Not that the gorillas were dirty: they groomed their long hair several times a day, which kept their glossy coats smooth and combed. And they sometimes assisted one another with the hard-to-reach parts. Other than that there was little physical contact among the adults, except when Queen Two and Queen Three engaged in one of their quarrels, which could degenerate into biting and pushing and screaming and hair pulling. But King could put a stop to that by glaring at the offenders and grunting sharply just once.

Strangely absent were loving gestures, except when one of the Queens rested her head on King's silver saddle as he slept. King's own contact with his wives was more inclined to light slaps or not-so-light shoves. And he always slept alone.

Although it was obvious that every gorilla in the family was genuinely fond of King, the big gorilla accepted all homage as his due; he never saw to the comfort of his family, and regarded the safety of the children as the sole responsibility of their mothers. Still, all of them—Jeremy included—followed wherever King led.

That is, Jeremy followed until that day when King took it into his dim brain to lead the little band away from the pleasant woods and up the mountainside to a dismal landscape where the weather was terrible. The move was mystifying. He had no sooner learned what to expect from the gorillas then they did the unexpected. As much as they loved the warm sunshine, they climbed up to the higher reaches where dank clouds hovered. As abundant as was the forage in the woods, they left it for the zone of heath where they had to alter their diet.

Up there the apes could extract the tender pith from the senecios and the lobelias, but Jeremy could find not even a frog to sustain himself. And just when he had become accustomed to his own private hunting preserve, too. Jeremy knew personally every tree, every burrow, every bird, every monkey in his small neighborhood. He was even able to make repeated use of the platforth beds he had constructed in the familiar trees.

Then, just when things were going so wonderfully well, he found himself following King up the mountain where there were no squirrels nor forest mice nor grass rats. Even the burrowing mole rats were left behind at the upper limit of the forest on the edges of the moors.

To separate himself from his family was a hard decision to make, especially because on the day he parted from them the gorillas were particularly lovable because they were especially miserable. They were always miserable when it rained.

The morning of that day dawned clear enough, but then mornings almost always dawned clear, with the sun's first rays slanting long shafts of brilliance between branchless trunks of giant trees, which transformed the forest into a vaulted cathedral. At midday the clouds usually moved in and then lingered until midafternoon when the sky cleared in preparation for the spectacle of the African sunset.

That morning was the last happy one he spent with them. It remained in his memory forever, growing brighter and shinier each time he reached into his past for it, took it out, and turned it over lovingly in his mind.

He set out to do a little hunting before the gorillas awakened. As always, he shivered in the chilly mist until his stiff muscles warmed with the exertion of sprinting along the forest floor. Beyond the grass was more forest, and from it a duiker emerged from the shadows and began nibbling the flowers. Out of habit he edged toward it, already stringing his bow, reaching for his arrow. Then he surprised himself by laughing aloud with sheer joy, with the rightness of a world that contained an animal so perfect. "Run, little duiker," he called softly; "I'll look for a frog instead."

In the days to come, when he was being stalked by the specter of starvation, he was to look back upon that

wood with a longing for its berries, its birds' eggs, its
voles and rats, and even the single mouthful of tender
flesh rendered by a bird that proved to be mostly bones
and feathers. He was to recall sticky feasts of honey,
and he was to wish that he had never gone adventuring
away from his forest.

He lingered too long: already the dew that lay upon
the meadow was sparkling in the sunlight. He ran in
the direction of last night's sleeping place, long, sinewy
legs pumping, long, tawny hair streaming behind
him.

When he arrived the gorillas were just getting
started. King was yawning, displaying his long black
teeth. The three Queens were waiting for their lord
and master to start moving out. Jack and Jill were
swinging hand over hand through the lowest branches
of a tree. But King waited. The infant was having its
breakfast; it had a grip on its mother's breast and was
sucking noisily. At one point in the feeding the baby
paused, and milk spilled from its overflowing mouth.

Milk! The one thing he missed. How long it had
been since he had tasted his favorite beverage! It was
in a Hima village, where his hosts had offered him a
gourd full of fresh milk from their Ankole longhorns.
He felt again the clean white creaminess of it slipping
over his tongue and down his throat, the comfort of it
in his stomach.

"Don't be a baby," he ordered himself; "if you
wanted milk you should have stayed where there were
cows."

Jeremy had watched lions nurse their cubs and hyenas nurse their pups. He had milked cows on the farm and had watched while the native women nursed their babies. There was nothing about this or any other mammalian function, including birth, that was unfamiliar to him. Yet he turned away his gaze from this maternal scene, feeling as uneasy as if he had been staring at a sister or at an aunt whose privacy he had invaded. He was so much a member of the family now that sometimes he got mixed up—either feeling like a gorilla himself or thinking of the gorillas as human.

When they all finally moved into the underbrush, the feeding was hurried and intense. In silence and with no wasted effort, the apes stripped vines and stuffed the leaves into their mouths like bouquets. They shoved in leafy thistle tops, prickles and all. They pushed food into their mouths with one hand while they were reaching for more with the other. Celery was peeled like corn, and the stems went in end first like asparagus. There was a great snapping of branches, uprooting of plants, ripping, tearing, plucking, peeling, shredding; rapid choosing and discarding, and a constant chewing without the usual rest periods between courses.

Somehow the gorillas knew, though Jeremy was still to find out, that today was the day to vacate the forest.

Perhaps they were beginning to travel because the baby was older. It had grown rapidly to an alert child whose eyes followed every movement. It could grasp its mother's hair and ride on her back. It even grabbed

leaves in passing and stuffed its mouth. It could crawl now, too, and moved away from its mother on all fours until she reached out to pull it back.

Everyone in the troop was interested in this little bundle of black hair with the tuft of white on its rump, but the mother still would allow no one to touch it. However, she could travel faster now, and travel they did, following at first those highways of the forest: buffalo trails.

They were a noisy band of animals that made their way up the steep slope on all fours, grabbing at whatever was handy to haul themselves up the incline.

Their general direction was, at first, at an oblique angle upward, which brought them to the bank of a stream. It was not a wide stream; anyone could leap across it easily, or they could spring to a partly submerged rock and then to the far bank. But not one of the gorillas was willing to try it—not even when Jeremy demonstrated. "Look, King, look!" he called, crossing back and forth over the water. But his behavior only seemed to frighten them further as if they feared for his safety.

King, after some dim deliberation, decided to proceed along the near bank of the stream. Naturally, the other gorillas followed him, Jeremy tagging along and feeling disgusted with such timidity. Because now they were proceeding straight up the mountainside, and the going was so tough that he needed his stick to help him along.

After a few hours the vegetation changed. The slope

was covered with low round senecios that looked like artichokes, and ancient towering tree senecios with scaly trunks that branched at the top with clusters of large leaves. Tall, spiky stalks of lobelia grew straight as poles. Huge tree heaths, twisted and gnarled with hundreds of years of living in the heights, drooped with lichen.

When Jeremy stopped to suck oxygen into his pained chest, he saw the clouds come moving in. They wrapped wispy fingers around everything, then settled down like a heavy white blanket. A drizzling rain blotted out the forest sounds and muffled the footfalls of the gorillas as they trod over beds of liverwort and moss.

The misty landscape looked mysterious, waiting in primeval silence. Jeremy was chilled by the cold drizzle even through his bush jacket. His socks had long since rotted to nothing, and his bare feet were clammy inside his boots. The breath left his mouth in puffs of condensation, and every time he jostled a fern or hanging moss, icy droplets showered down his neck.

The drizzle turned suddenly into a heavy downpour, which soon became hail. When hailstones the size of marbles pelted the heads and backs of the apes, they stopped to huddle beneath the protection of a tree. Queen One found a fallen log on which to sit, hunched over. King walked over to where she sat and gave her a rude shove. The old female obligingly moved over to the end of the log, giving King all the space he needed.

The long hairs on King's arms were soaked. Water

dripped off his massive brow ridges and splashed on his muzzle. His eyes held an expression of misery. He sneezed twice, and gave a barking cough. He's caught cold, thought Jeremy; we'll all catch our death up here. What a stupid idea this was.

The new mother now crept to the log where sat Queen One and King. The baby was clinging to her hair and her big arm was shielding it from the hail. King gave Queen One a second rough push, which bumped her heavily off the end of the log, whereupon the young female took the Queen's vacated place. Queen One then crawled on all fours to where the other two females were huddled together with Jack on one lap and Jill on the other.

Jeremy watched this little tableau with interest. On more than one occasion he had noticed that the new mother was the favorite wife of King, receiving what meager favors the head of the family had to bestow. But he also suspected that the aged Queen One was accustomed to more consideration from her mate than she had been getting, and that the number one position in the lineup of wives had been appropriated by the young wife only since she had given birth.

The old gray-haired female had eyes so wise and kind and sad-looking that Jeremy sometimes felt a rush of affection for her. It vaguely disturbed him that whenever he glanced at her she was regarding him with some sort of gorilla emotion: intense but, to him, unfathomable. This she was doing now. Jeremy moved over to where she sat and put a hand on her arm. She

124

stared at the hand. Slowly she lifted her eyes and was, it seemed, about to look directly at him when she turned her head aside. She held her body motionless until the hail turned back into rain and the rain stopped altogether.

Staying where they were, they gave over this afternoon's rest period to attending to their coats, for their hair was sodden. Jeremy's bush jacket had to be hung on the limb of a tree to dry.

The gorillas examined and scratched every inch of their bodies, parting the hair and inspecting the skin like nearsighted people searching intently for tiny imperfections. They looked so serious about it that Jeremy had to stifle a laugh. "They really are a comical bunch," he said to himself. "I'll miss them most awfully. But I'll be back just as soon as I collect enough meat to last while we're all living up here." The idea of a permanent separation did not occur to him.

Now the females were bending down the stalks of senecios and ripping off the leafy tops, plucking ferns from moss, pulling up roots from the soaked earth. But instead of moving about with each going her own way, they stayed within viewing distance of one another as if they, too, felt the alien atmosphere of this place. King simply stayed seated and reached out an arm to whatever edibles were handy.

Jack and Jill, having assured themselves that the grownups would remain in sight, felt confident enough to play. They invented a new game: one youngster pulled himself up a steep muddy bank on all fours, then slid down on his bottom. The other one followed. Up they went, slipping and skidding; down they slid while emitting soft panting chuckles. Their mouths were partly open with the corners drawn back in a smile. Whenever the slider collided with the climber, the two came down together as one furry body.

Tiring of that game, they picked the mud off one another's backs and started another, their favorite. Each caught hold of a hanging liana and swung back and forth, kicking the hind legs wildly in the air.

Little Jack swung into the back of his mother, pitching her forward onto the cold ground that was still covered with hailstones. The Queen picked herself up and resumed her feeding, being accustomed to the high-spirited roughhouse of the youngsters. Then, having managed one direct hit, Jack launched himself at Jeremy the next time around, but his target ducked soon enough to avoid being likewise sent sprawling.

Jeremy watched for a few minutes. This looked like fun. He caught hold of a liana, tested its strength with a strong tug, and swung—looping back and forth, up and back, higher and higher, kicking at protruding branches. He felt weightless and free, powerful and wildly joyous.

Queen One was looking up at him, a puzzled expression in her bleary eyes. She seemed perturbed at his strange actions. And even Jeremy himself was struck with wonderment that he was "carrying on like a kid." At the same time, though, he had a feeling of finality: as if this silly romp with the little apes was somehow his last crazy fling, and that the free wild joy of the swaying liana was the climax of a vanishing childhood.

Then, while the family was busy, he picked up his jacket and his wooden spear and strolled away through a rising mist high on the mountain where puddles of ice lay in depressions and the fallen leaves were crisp with frost.

Chapter Eight

A Hut for a Hermit

He told himself that his reason for climbing to the top of the volcano was to survey the surrounding area and to get his bearings, but it was really curiosity to see what was up there.

He climbed over wet and slippery rocks, over outcrops of lava, over springy mats of sodden moss that slipped beneath his feet and pitched him forward. He grabbed handholds of frosty moss that gave way and sent him sliding backward on his stomach. By the time he had climbed in and out of the countless deep ravines that radiated down from the summit, he began to wish he had stayed where he was. Then a sudden shower drenched him.

A flash of lightning lit the whole visible sky, followed by a deep roll of thunder that lasted several seconds. Rain came down in huge drops that fell straight to the ground; and all around was nothing but dull uniform gray. He could not distinguish objects more than five feet from his eyes, yet he knew he was in a forest of tall trees when he should, by this time, be above the timberline.

Then he began to wonder whether darkness had fallen early, for he was entombed in blackness in a place of tangled creepers, dripping foliage, ropy vines, and sheet upon sheet of falling water whose continuous sound would have drowned out any other. There could be no thought of sitting down in that awful gloom where neither vision nor hearing could function to alert him to approaching danger. So he went on.

As suddenly as it began, the rain turned itself off and the grayness lightened. But now fog lay upon his face. It obscured his path and silenced his footfalls, making him feel disembodied or as though his feet were not touching the ground. This floating sensation was heightened by a lightheadedness that made him want to surrender his lead-weight body to a springy mat of foot-deep moss. But he kept on, afraid to be overtaken by night while he was still working his way over the outcrops of lava.

He was out of the forest, and traveling over scrubby bushes. After a time he felt himself on naked rock. He had reached the summit.

There was an enormous hole in the earth. It was about a mile across, and about a thousand feet deep. Inside it was a heaving sea of black lava which parted here and there to reveal burning orange-red liquid: a cauldron of hideous porridge with great bubbles swelling and bursting on its surface. The cindery rim was hot against him as he gazed down, past sheer walls and ledges that spurted steam, into the pit of seething black stuff that roiled and belched. He wondered that it was all so silent.

"My God," he whispered, "it's the fiery furnace; the

bottomless pit; the place called hell." He gave a long whistle. "Wizard! A real live volcano." He could not stop staring into it. It held him hypnotized.

He recalled that the Bahunde—a tribe that cultivates the flanks of these volcanoes—have a belief that the interior of the volcanoes is inhabited by the ghosts of their dead ancestors, and that whenever men fight among themselves those ghosts shake the mountain and stir the fires, throwing up burning cinders and pouring hot lava down the slopes. "Huh," he said, "I'll wager those old ghosts never get any rest. I wonder if they know what's going on in Kenya right now."

His mind finally came back to practical matters. This was the wrong mountain, of course; he knew that as soon as he saw the fire in the crater. Somehow he had managed to climb either Mount Nyamuragira or Mount Nyiragongo, the two westernmost volcanoes that erupt every two years or so. He could see the other volcanoes lying close by, and he could see now that the two hot ones are connected to the six dormant ones across a high saddle. It was across that saddle that he had come.

"Well, now you've done it. You're miles—about ten miles, I'd judge—from where you want to be. It must have been the rain and the fog, or the way those ridges slant and go off at angles. What an idiot I was for not using my compass!"

Immediately, though, his irritation with himself was forgotten. A strong southwestern wind had come up and pushed the rain clouds off to the east, washing the western sky with the tender lucid blue that always comes after a violent tropical storm has cleared the air. And there to the north was revealed the mighty range of Mountains of the Moon. For one breathtaking moment the jagged rocky cliffs with their shining white glaciers were revealed in all their grandeur. In another moment all was cloaked in clouds as if it had been a mirage.

To the west the Congo Basin stretched to the horizon. To the north was Lake Edward; to the south, Lake Kivu; to the east were the six new-washed volcanoes. He was standing on Africa's great divide where the headwaters of the Congo River and those of the Nile River are only ten miles apart. He was straddling the great spine of Africa.

This should have been a timeless place, as remote and hushed as the bottom of the sea. It should have been a place surrounded only by wild and savage country and inhabited by no one but native Africans— as it was before Henry Stanley found it and nearly died of starvation and exposure on these volcanoes.

But Jeremy had seen that the lakes were lined with resorts. Even now, Europeans were down there swimming, sailing, water skiing, and drinking at little tables beneath crystal chandeliers. He could almost hear the whine of motorboats, the wail of saxophones: the sounds of white Africa. Jazz combos instead of jungle drums. "Crazy. Africa is a crazy place," he said, and looked up to where a lone eagle soared overhead, wheeled, swooped, and flew straight toward a nest on top of one of the volcanoes. Then the mountain darkened with that suddenness with which the African night descends.

On the practical side, there was one advantage to spending the night on this bald crest of volcanic rock: if the volcano decided to explode he would be the first to know it. He crawled under a rock overhang which protected him from the blasting wind, and from where he could see the crater glowing with an orange light. It was his private campfire, provided by the god of the mountain so that he would not freeze. He felt like the first man on earth—or the last. Either way, it was lonely.

He thought of the gorillas. "Those old apes have made beds and gone to sleep without a thought of me, I'll wager." Jeremy longed for the gorillas, even though he knew that if he lived with them all his life they would never miss him the way he missed them at this moment: his first solitary sleep since he met them. Then he fell into a deep dreamless sleep.

Exhausted from the long day and the climb, he did not awaken until the sun broke clear of the volcanoes. He could think of nothing but his hunger, plan no further than his next meal. He would not find it on this freshly erupted lava rock which supported nothing except a few cushions of tiny yellow flowers that bloomed courageously in a sheltered hollow, living like himself on a very small margin of safety.

A few hours' walk straight downhill would bring him to Lake Kivu and one of the Europeans' playgrounds where a gay holiday crowd would be fishing and diving from rafts, or eating a leisurely breakfast of rolls with butter, coffee with milk, porridge, tea. . . . But no; heading for one of the dormant volcanoes, he descended the slope across lava fields sparsely covered with lichens, grasses, and ferns.

Upon the mountain lay a thick, woolly silence that caused him to think his hearing had failed. The sun beat down relentlessly. He took off his shirt, only to put it on again when he walked through a patch of nettles that stung his chest and left raised welts that itched and burned like fury.

Now he was treading upon the level terrain of a connecting saddle—which one he did not care, because he knew that he was back in gorilla country. At least this was the sort of forest in which gorillas might be expected to live, for it contained plenty of forage and nest-making material. Besides, he felt relaxed now that he was back inside the forest reserve and gorilla sanctuary. And just as long as he did not stray again, he would be as snug and private as he wanted to be. As private as a Pygmy.

As he trudged along, his thoughts were occupied with the idea of a government that provides a sanctuary for endangered animals but none for endangered humans—like himself. Africa has parks for elephant and lion and antelope; it has refuges for waterfowl. But where is there a refuge for humans who need to escape a crazy world? Where is there even a single isolated mountaintop set aside for people? "Take this forest preserve, now: fine; but how about preserving one Jeremy Jenkins? Well anyway, here I am and the joke is on everybody. Bully!" He swung his body in circles.

Even if there were no gorillas on the volcanoes, the natives would avoid these heights because they need their hothouse climate down in the sultry valley. Too, they are terrified of the sudden snowstorms that come out of nowhere, and believe that such storms are the revenge of the jealous and wrathful god that lives up here.

Jeremy was thinking about the cold, about the way the gorillas don't mind it at all. It's that thick coat of hair they have, he decided. You don't find all that hair on a lowland gorilla down in the Congo Basin; they are separate races. Maybe some of the Congo ones got trapped in the east by a river or something, and cut off from the others. More likely, with the "locals" farming all the land around these mountains the gorillas were forced up to the cold parts.

"People!" he said with disgust. "They're pushing animals right off the earth. My gorillas have no place to go." Then he stopped in his tracks and struck his forehead. "I must be getting balmy! All I can think about now is gorillas. Before I came up here I didn't know where gorillas live, and didn't much care. Now I'm always worrying about the poor dumb things. And what in blazes am I doing, anyway? Tracking gorillas."

He knew what to look for: trampled vegetation,

branches broken by strong hands, knuckle prints or footprints in the earth, and beds—preferably fresh beds containing fresh dung. Because gorillas never bother getting up at night or even first thing in the morning, their nests are always soiled—which may be the reason why they never sleep in the same bed twice.

He sat on a log to contemplate his situation, rest a while, make plans for the night. He would not want to spend it sprawled on this moldy floor.

He suffered from such hunger that he feared death by starvation. It was an emptiness that would not be satisfied with small edible roots and bulbs, berries, or drops of congealed gum. When he saw huge white grubs in the rotten wood of a fallen tree he considered eating them as the Pygmies do. But the look of them disgusted him. A chap could starve to death here, he thought, and his body be used to fertilize those orchids that are wrapped around the trees, or these impatiens, or—

Suddenly the silence was shattered by a shrill shriek that made drops of sweat stand out on his forehead. It was a scream so loud, so piercing, so unearthly, that it was like a blow on the head. When his heart started beating again it thumped in his chest.

That outcry could have been made only by a person who was being murdered—or by a gorilla. Yes: it was a male gorilla that had bellowed forth that high-pitched barking scream. Jeremy laughed uproariously. He laughed so hard that he rolled off the log onto the ground and kept on rolling himself around, guffawing like a madman. Anybody else who heard that scream would be terrified. But to Jeremy that outrageous shriek meant that although he was still lost, he was no longer alone. With renewed energy, he went on.

It was toward evening that he came across the stone wall. And even when he realized what it was, he had trouble believing his eyes.

It had been made by human hands: the first sign of human intrusion he had seen up here. And it was a closed rectangle of rough and jagged lava rock, built to define a grave.

Whose grave this was he could not determine— whether missionary or explorer or mountain climber or just a hermit like himself. But the person buried here must have been a Christian, because more lava rock had been laid out upon the ground roughly in the shape of a Saint George's cross.

The grave was in the corner of a large open meadow. And in the center of that meadow was a hut —a crude cabin made of rough horizontal boards nailed together.

The sight of that hut caused in him mixed feelings. He was not at all sure that he was ready to re-enter the world of humans. If he were to leave this place right now and continue on his way, he would remain as solitary as he wished to be and for as long as he liked. But if he were to explore further, he might come upon another human being. In the end his curiosity got the better of him.

Anyway, it was not likely that anyone lived here. The two iron barrels placed beneath the roof to catch rainwater were rusted completely away. The tin roof had slipped and it hung at a rakish angle. The door of the outhouse had fallen off and the outhouse was a ruin.

Inside was a fireplace and a supply of dry wood which almost filled the small space. Otherwise there was a dense network of spiderwebs; and there was the sort of baking heat that is held in by a tin roof. No African would live beneath a metal roof when thatching provides snug warmth at night and cool shade in the day, and mats more tightly with each rain. No native would feel the need of an outhouse in this wilderness, either, much less an outhouse with a door. No, this rough board hut had sheltered a European. And it could not have been put here, he was positive, more recently than about twenty-three years ago. For it was that long ago that the Belgian king, Albert, had set aside the Virunga Volcanoes as a sanctuary for gorillas, adding it to the rest of Parc Albert. Then later it became also a forest reserve.

Who would want to live up here? Nobody but himself. And even he, who left no traces of his presence, was constantly aware that it is forbidden to be in the park.

Not that he worried about being found out. Anyone who could elude the Mau Mau, not to mention the Kenya police and the British authorities, could certainly keep from being discovered by the two or three park guards who were supposed to patrol the international borders of this reserve once a year.

"Don't be silly. This is just an old abandoned shack that nobody knows is here." He told himself to relax.

But, as old as this shack was, he noticed when he set about making a fire that the firewood had been cut and stacked recently, and the hearth, which should have been filled with debris, was not.

Someone had occupied this hut within the past few years. Perhaps a poacher. Perhaps the guard on one of his anual trips. If so—a new and exciting hope was born—there might be a cache of food. A frantic search did indeed reveal a carton partly filled with some tins of meat and some of beans—enough to last for weeks. There was also the ultimate luxury, a tin box almost full of tea.

"Bully! White man's food! Did I say there are no gods on this mountain?" With that, he did a few leaps into the air and shook his shoulders in imitation of a Masai war dance. Now, with the dented kettle he found in the corner, there was everything a person needed except only the water for the tea.

When he went outside to look for a stream the sky had turned an ominous gray color. Then the snow began, swirling and stinging like needles. "Forget the stream," he told himself; "I'll make my tea with snowflakes. Forget the storm; I'll get a good fire going. Just like old times. Just like home. Almost."

Back in the cabin he began opening tins with his knife and greedily feeding his hunger, all the while holding a silent conversation with himself in the belief that a good meal is worthy of good talk.

On the one hand, he thought, there is a lot to be said for the way he had been living: the easy, careless life of a nomadic hunter-gatherer; living off the land like a Pygmy or a Bushman or an Australian aborigine; hunting and fishing and gathering whatever nature provided; dwelling in the forest like a young Tarzan with a troop of friendly apes for company; surviving in the wilds by means of his own cunning, and existing in perfect harmony with the dumb creatures of the wood. At least he did not have to answer to anyone, nor did he have to involve himself in the affairs of the civilized world, which seemed to have gone quite mad of late.

On the other hand, an occasional tin of beans and meat, an occasional drink of tea, a sleep beneath a real roof in a room warm and bright with fire—these inventions of civilization, he had to admit, he was enjoying immensely. And now that he was being truthful with himself, he also had to admit that the prospect of hunger and darkness had seemed intolerable to him when he was contemplating this night in the black forest with its strange moving shadows, its weird rustling sounds, and no sleeping gorillas for company.

While the wind howled and blew swirling snow around the cabin, Jeremy said a silent prayer to whatever spirit had guided his footsteps this way.

That night, as he looked back on it in the days to come, was a turning point in the idyllic life he had made for himself on the mountain. He had parted from his precious gorillas and had climbed to the summit where his senses, heightened by hunger, were overwhelmed by the sight of a fire-breathing crater and by vast vistas of mountains and forests—and by the idea of Africa's wild and unexplored areas lying so close to the water-skiing, sailboating tourists on the lakes. Then he was abruptly brought back to civilized surroundings: this cabin, this food. It was probably the sum of all these experiences in the short space of two days that had the effect of shaking something loose in his mind.

Now, sitting by the roaring fire, fed and warm and rested for the first time, he faced—for the first time— the certainty that he would have to go back. It would take him about ten days, he estimated, to walk down the mountain and across southwestern Uganda, arriving in the town of Entebbe, the seat of Uganda's colonial government. There was a British military post there where he could report his presence among the living. That is, if he wanted to. . . .

"I'll think about it tomorrow." His eyes closed as the effects of the food and the fire combined to lull him into drowsiness. "And I suppose I shall have to go back. But there's no hurry about it."

That night he had a dream. The gorillas were being chased by a horde of natives with spears. Higher and higher up the mountain ran the apes in an effort to escape their pursuers. King and the three Queens, the young mother with her infant, Jack and Jill, all stumbling up the steep slope and slipping on the frosty moss and sliding backward, striving to reach the summit. Then they were there, scrambling up the rocks, still encircled by shouting, spear-brandishing natives. Just as the gorillas were about to go over the hot, cindery rim of the yawning crater, Jeremy awoke in a dripping sweat and moved away from the scorching heat of his fire.

Chapter Nine

Only Gods and Gorillas

At such a great height, and this close to the equator, people tend to go a little insane sometimes. It is the effect of the oxygen-thin atmosphere and the way the sun's rays are directed with a clear brilliance—the raw ultraviolet seeming to burn into the brain the way it burns into the skin. Add to this an enormous silence, complete solitude, a measure of fasting, and you have a person grown either slightly mad or exceptionally sane.

For months on end the only human voice Jeremy had heard was his own, and even that seldom broke the forest silence with more than a whisper. But since he had been eating and sleeping in the cabin he had taken to muttering to the bones buried in the far corner of the meadow.

Each morning he would nod toward the grave with a "Jambo"—the Masai greeting used in East Africa. Sometimes it was "Jambo, George," for Saint George of the cross.

Jeremy was now convinced that this hut had been occupied neither by a park guard on his rounds nor by a poacher checking his traps, but by a white man. Everything indicated it. A white man had come up these slopes bringing a supply of food—his intention, no doubt, being to live here in peace and contemplation. Surely no more beautiful spot could be found than this meadow of grass and flowers surrounded by forests, with the conical volcanoes rising like pyramids all around. It was a marvelous place in which to live but a terrible place in which to die.

Poor George. All alone.

A scene reconstructed itself in his mind. Someone—doubtless an African—came upon this cabin, pushed open the door, and was confounded by the sight of a body: perhaps wasted away with fever, already black with decay. An ages-old impulse gave the intruder the will to drag the object far from the hut, to excavate a pit. The gruesome task was not finished until rocks were laid upon the grave to keep the ghost from drifting about; the lava stone wall was further insurance against a wandering spirit.

Then the passerby, who had no business being here in the first place, fled the haunted spot, carrying away nothing that had belonged to the poor devil who forgot that to live alone is to die alone, with no man to say a burial service for a mournful skeleton.

It is the custom for Africans to burn to the ground any hut in which someone has died, and with it everything touched by the stricken owner, believing such things to be cursed by the power of evil that has been unleashed. Another custom is to bury the possessions of the corpse in the grave. Jeremy was thankful every day that this cabin of weathered boards was no flimsy thatch-roofed grass hut, easily fired; and thankful, too, that his precious store of tinned food had not been wasted in a hole in the ground.

"Whoever you are," he addressed the silent bones in the corner of the meadow, "I thank you for the food."

Had poor George been a fugitive from the gallows, or a fugitive from civilization? A criminal, or a philosopher?

Whoever he was, he had provided himself with a goodly supply of split logs as if he feared (or knew for certain) that he would not be able to get out for a long while. But, because the wood was very dry, and because Jeremy made generous fires every night, the stacks of split logs dwindled rapidly.

"Someone made off with your ax, you know," he informed George. "You must have left it lying about outside. Careless. Now I have to build this fire with brush." And he made trip after trip into the forest, dragging back enormous loads of twigs and branches.

He thought often of the nights he might have passed on this mountain, alone, without fire, and with his imagination falling prey to the strange gloom of a forest inhabited by sinister shadows: vague dark shapes that moved in a shifty way as if they were watching him. An owl, a bat, a nightjar, or a huge moth—each shadowy form had been a menacing demon or spirit during those black hours he had spent in the branches of a tree. He admitted to himself that if the gorillas had not been sleeping above and below him he could not have stuck it out.

Before he had the company of this friendly hearth, willed to him by the previous squatter, he would listen for the coarse mournful crying of hyenas, the sudden shrill scream of a hyrax that always sounds like a tragedy in the night, and the sickening cough of the leopard that can be heard in the hundred other mysterious, frightening night noises. But now he had a night light, and the flames of his fire freed him of the worst of his private nightmares.

First, those specters that used to come to his tree platform as soon as the darkness dropped upon the mountain were now held at bay by the cheerful glow. Also, those shadows that flickered and danced upon the walls changed from the menacing black shapes of panga-flourishing Mau Mau to the wildly gyrating figures of dancing Pygmies, leaping and twirling about the campfire in an orgy of joy and praise for the life-giving forest.

And many nights Jeremy danced, too. He danced naked with the flickering shadows on the cabin walls, flinging himself about, twisting and whirling as the Pygmies did in an abandoned dance of life and the love of life, of joy and exaltation; rejoicing in his free, wild spirit.

He would have stayed in the cabin longer except that eventually the food cartons were empty. It was not that he had given up hunting, only that he was seldom able to catch anything. That, he realized, was because his hunting had lost its former urgency. When hunger had spurred him on, his eye had been accurate, his ears keen, his nose as sensitive as an animal's. Now those senses—heightened over the months by need— had degenerated in that hut cozy with firelight and provisions. The little green tree frog remained where it was, amongst its camouflage of green leaves, instead of falling to his stone missile. Clearly the time had come to quit this seductive place where he had so easily succumbed to the soft luxurious trappings of civilization.

For his farewell dinner he had saved one portion of tea which he planned to savor slowly by his final fire. Then he would tidy the cabin, bury the empty tins, and be on his way back to where he knew the gorillas would be. They were such creatures of habit that their path was predictable, and their home range was a small area on the southward-facing slope of a nearby volcano.

He went into the woods carrying his dented kettle. But because the day was young he strolled along the stream to where a still pool eddied away from the main current. Leaning over the pool to drink, he saw reflected on its surface a face he did not recognize. It was an image that refused to merge with his own. This gaunt, hollow-cheeked apparition with long matted hair could have nothing to do with that other fellow: the fresh-faced young schoolboy from a Kenya farm.

Living in a high equatorial altitude not only causes

intermittent madness, it also•causes people to age rapidly. Even at the seven thousand feet of the White Highlands, the Europeans (usually the women) refer in a half-jesting way to their ravaged complexions, to the bloom that was borne off on the dry winds of the high country. So it was not surprising that here on the volcanoes, at twice the altitude of the Highlands, Jeremy had aged.

As he walked slowly back, dangling his still empty kettle, he set to wondering just how long he had been on the mountain. Long enough, surely, for his wrists to grow out of his jacket sleeves, his boots to pinch his feet, his hair to reach down his back. Long enough, too, he thought, to be cured of the sickness he had contracted from civilization. Now that he was truly alive, he realized that for the past several years he had been going through the motions of living, like a sleepwalker. He had been existing in a paralysis of fear, and it was possible that, during those years, his development had been stunted by that paralysis, and that his new freedom had released him into new growth. He felt now that his mind had burst its bonds the way his clothes had burst their seams.

Back at the meadow he flung his arms wide to take in the volcanoes, the forest, the blue sky. His estate. He had been matured by it and had come into his full bloom. The silence and the stillness of the mountains had crept inside him, and wherever he went from here it would remain with him. The mountains had given him a measure of their strength and their peace. Perhaps not the amount of strength and peace the gorillas had, but enough so that he could take up the existence of a man among men.

Departing from the meadow he bid farewell to his benefactor, George, the mountain hermit who, like himself, had run away. Speaking in tones loud enough to be heard below ground he called:

"Hey, you down there! Listen! It's no good, old chap. Only gods and gorillas can live up here!" He liked the sound of it. "Only gods and gorillas!" he shouted again, this time for his own benefit because, having raised his voice for the first time, he was surprised to hear it sounding deeper than he remembered.

Then, as he followed the stream on its downward course, he was struck with the thought that he was like that stream that has its spring on the mountain peak but whose purpose it is to mingle with the river. He had found his source on the mountain. Now he would stop resisting the idea of going down the mountainside, of mingling with the river of humanity. If that was his purpose.

But first he had to find the gorillas—and find some he did. But they were not *his* gorillas, and he found them with startling suddenness.

With all possible stealth he followed a trail of fresh knuckle prints that led in all directions in the usual way of gorilla trails. He knew he was hard on their heels, but no crackling or snapping sounds warned him that he was getting close. He lifted his eyes from the trail to confront the huge shining blackness of a big male, half crouching, half standing in a thicket. The beast fastened Jeremy with a fixed stare, which hardened into a glare. Jeremy's knees buckled.

One of the oldest bits of gorilla lore is that, confronted with a gorilla at close range, one must stand one's ground and look the animal in the eye. To turn one's back and flee is to invite a charge and a bite on the seat—or worse. So goes the gorilla lore. Jeremy had no intention of turning his back or of fleeing: he knew how fast these animals can run; he knew the power in those arms and the length of those teeth. He wanted to do the right thing, if only he could be sure what that was. There was no margin for error here.

One thing Jeremy had learned for himself was that it is a mistake to look a gorilla in the eye. Despite what everyone says, a direct stare aimed at a gorilla is received as a suggestion of hostility, a threat. He was on the receiving end of just such a stare right now; the piercing look he was getting from those hard, glinty brown eyes could not be mistaken for anything but a warning: Be off! Or else! The creature was rising to its full height.

With a wit quicker than conscious thought, Jeremy swiveled his head from side to side the way King did the day the elephant came. He was careful not to let his eyes rest on the gorilla's eyes; careful, too, to stand firm even though his impulse was to beat a hasty retreat. The temper of this strange beast was the unknown factor in this face-to-face encounter, and universal among both animals and men is fear born of suspicion of the stranger.

One short, sharp grunt from the gorilla gave rise to a rustling in the surrounding bushes. There were others. How many others? Are they retreating or advancing? Jeremy waited. Then came the hoot, accompanied by the sound of cupped palms beaten on the chest. And the teeth! Suddenly, and without a sound, the black figure disappeared as if swallowed up by the bushes. Jeremy climbed the nearest tree.

From there he could see some of the others. There were a lot of them, coming and going. Several females and some youngsters gathered around his tree, craning their necks, shoving each other aside to get a better view. They were more curious than frightened, and most of them lost interest after the first excitement and went on about their business—except for the leader, the original hooter and chest-beater who kept a wary eye on the stranger, and two black-haired males, who roared and beat their chests.

It was these two young adult males that interested Jeremy the most, for he had never seen a totally black male gorilla. These two were on the verge of developing a silver saddle, for a few silvery hairs had sprouted on their backs. When they roared, their voices squeaked and cracked, trailing off on a high pitch. They were obviously adolescent, halfway between a child like Jack and an adult like King. And although the big male was clearly dominant over the entire troop, these two almost-grown males lorded it over the females, who moved aside for them.

As long as the troop stayed near his tree he was trapped. But he was back in gorilla country—"where I belong," as he put it. Despite the hostility he was receiving, he was with his sort of animal. Sitting there in the tree, virtually unable to move, observing the movements of these tense and sensitive animals, a new and unexpected realization burst upon him.

Ever since he was big enough to lift a gun he had been bent upon killing wild animals. With no thought for their right to go on living he had brought to their knees bushbuck, impala, Thomson's gazelle, Grant's gazelle. He had watched men shoot elephant, leopard, lion; he himself had shot dozens of hyenas and baboons, knocking them flat with one bullet. How casually he had cut the skin from the still quivering flesh of a zebra that, until a few seconds before, was galloping with its herd. And how easily he had used his gun to supply buffalo meat to those natives who wanted it. None of those animals he killed so cleverly and at such a safe distance was ever a threat to people, and only the hyenas and leopards ever threatened the farm animals.

He closed his eyes and visualized the taxidermy shop in Nairobi where there are crouching leopards and lions and lionesses posed with their mouths open to display the teeth and make them look as fierce as possible. They look almost alive, but they are skins stretched over plaster forms. All were killed by lawful hunters, yet none was needed for meat; they are people's stuffed toys. When he tried to imagine these gorillas stuffed, frozen in their postures like a photograph, his mind did a somersault. He saw the skins of people stretched over plaster forms, all carefully posed in postures intended to look natural. To look natural, each would have to be holding a weapon. . . .

He must have dozed off, because the troop had moved along. He left his tree to keep them in sight because he had no intention of passing this night alone when he could have the sort of company he was used to.

That night was spent lying in an old gorilla bed about halfway up in a tree. Not a small and lofty bed such as that built by a youngster, nor a huge low-down one made by a big male, but something in between: one built by a female. The selection of a bed made him think of the story of the three bears, and he went to sleep hungry but happy.

While the forest still lay silent under the fading stars, he crept from his bed. In semi-darkness he walked through the forest. He picked and ate handfuls of big, fluffy pink mushrooms, fresh and firm. When his stomach could hold no more, he made little packages of them by tearing large leaves from the undergrowth and hitching them to his belt, using the stems of the leaves for twine the way the Pygmies taught him to do it.

In a mountain stream where water slid icy cold over black rocks, he doused himself; then, shivering in the chilly dawn, he dressed in a hurry and started running along a path made by forest animals. He was heading downhill across a saddle toward another volcano, following wherever possible the wide buffalo trails and the narrow antelope trails.

He did not find the gorillas that day or the next. He started to worry that they were lost to him forever; and this forest was frightening, populated as it was with leopards and with buffalo, which is the most dangerous animal in Africa. If startled at a distance, buffalo will flee, but at close range they charge. And even the antelope can use its sharp horns like twin daggers if a mother is defending a baby. So he kept his spear sharpened and he made as much noise as possible, singing and shouting and incidentally enjoying the sound of his new, deeper voice.

From time to time he stopped to listen for the sound of a gorilla roar, or a bark, or a chest-thumping. Once he shouted "King!" but from the depths of the woods came only an echo of his own voice. The park guard back in Goma had said that if you call the gorilla by name you will never find it. Silly superstition! Or was it?

Before dusk on the second day the forest darkened and a shower of leaves and branches came spinning to the ground. Rain came down so hard it hurt, after which all was blackness.

Daybreak brought release in the form of action. The forest was barely illuminated when he set off for the place where he had last seen the gorillas: the zone of senecios and heather. They would not still be there, nor would there be any footprints left in the wet moss. But he had seen the way the gorillas break off the lobelia stalks, and it was these traces he looked for when he came to the volcano which had been his home.

The closer he got the faster he ran, whipping around trees, leaping across logs, and laughing aloud when he came to the stream which King had refused to cross. The stream was now swollen with yesterday's heavy rain, rushing fast where its course was clear and spreading out on soggy banks where obstacles held it back. In some places the vegetation was too dense to penetrate, but even when he detoured around these places he was careful not to stray from the sound of running water.

The sun was high and brilliant when he stopped to rest and eat the last of the mushrooms. A quiet joy filled him now, a satisfying peace. He was feeling the relaxation a of person who has finally arrived home after a long journey. It was not that he had traveled a far distance as measured by kilometers, nor had he been away for more than a couple of months. But he knew that he was a different person from the boy who lived here before. Something had happened to him while he was living in that cabin, although he was not certain what it was.

Anyway, he was sleepy now and even though it was not yet noon he slept for several hours, making up for his sleepless night of waiting in the dark, wet forest. He awoke with a shaft of sunlight full upon his face, a single beam of it having found him through the leaves as if to remind him of his mission.

Continuing downhill he came upon one familiar sight after another: the glade where he used to sit among the tree ferns; the meadow where he saw the duiker and let it get away; the clearing where the blackberries always grew. He stopped to stuff himself with berries. He felt the familiar burn and sting of nettles which he knew would make his legs itch for hours, but he did not mind because he was home.

He was following a familiar buffalo trail. So careless was he now, so reckless in his movements, that he flung himself sideways just in time to avoid stepping into a trap!

Chapter Ten

Rites of Passage

Poachers! There had never been any sign of poachers on this slope before.

"The devils!" He started to spit out curses—curses he was not even aware that he knew. "May their children be carried off by hyenas. May their families fall sick from a spell. May their crops rot, and may they rot too—their ancestors be defiled by dogs—" until he realized that he was repeating traditional Kikuyu curses, and in the Kikuyu language. They were curses of the sort intended to bring calamity down upon entire families, entire clans.

He stopped at once because, whatever he told himself about African superstitions, he half believed in the power of the spoken curse used as he was using it, to punish evil. Having seen with his own eyes entire Kikuyu families ruined by one potent curse, having seen people actually sicken and die from one magic spell, he feared that he had unleashed something supernatural.

"Hold on there," he cautioned himself. Weren't you told that smugglers avoid the customs posts by using a route across one of these mountain saddles: the one between Uganda and Ruanda? And didn't the villagers say that they had the boundary line of the reserve raised from the eight-thousand to the nine-thousand-

156

foot level so that more fields could be planted? And don't forget all that illegal cutting that goes on down where the natives get those green bamboo stems for making baskets. What's to stop them?

But a trap! He clenched his teeth and looked around. This forest is mine! —and the gorillas', he remembered to add. Nobody is allowed to come up here and set a trap to break a duiker's leg. Nobody is allowed to disturb my gorillas in their own forest and make them afraid of people. Afraid of *me!*

That was it: worse even than the idea of a mangled duiker was the idea of King and the others learning to fear *him,* discovering that he was one of *Them.* He imagined his gorillas turning on him accusing eyes, casting him out with hooting and chest-beating as though he were a stranger. "No," he said aloud to the trap. "That must not happen."

Now he was searching for something. On that day when King and the troop moved out of this wood, some impulse made Jeremy hang his knapsack on a tree limb and leave it there. He certainly could have used that tattered old canvas sack when he was gathering all those mushrooms. But, left here, it became his flag, his banner: marking the fort and holding it for his return.

He found it. And he found old gorilla nests, too: made, he knew, by none other than his own family, which gave them a sort of sentiment. And here was one of his own platform beds, needing a bit of repairing but still usable with the addition of some leaves. As if it were his childhood cot, he settled down on it with a sense of relief, for night had fallen.

Never had he slept so late. The day was foggy and overcast, which meant a hard search for the gorillas. He strained his hearing through the small forest noises to make out the ones he longed to hear: a cough, a belch, a squeal—anything that would lead him to them. Now that he had seen that awful trap he was afraid to call aloud; the poacher might be along to check it today. He cursed the fog that filled his eyes with cloying, clammy damp.

Step by careful step he trod the trail, feeling his way so as to avoid a trap or a snare. He did not want to be hung up by one leg like an unlucky antelope that steps on a wire noose, triggering a bent sapling to snap up, then waiting for a hunter to finish him off, or just dying there, picked at by vultures and maggots.

Although the day was especially cool, he was sweating; but not from exertion nor even from fear of making a wrong step. The perspiration that beaded his face and ran down his sides came from some nameless apprehension. It was as if he had a premonition of trouble—some kind of trouble caused by an outside evil that had insinuated itself into his forest while he was away.

Some people are afraid of gorillas. But Jeremy had become afraid of humans—afraid of the things that humans can do to the innocent and the unarmed. He had acquired the instincts of a wild and wary animal. Even the leopard held fewer terrors for him than a spear-carrying native looking for sport . . . or for meat.

"Those natives never did respect boundaries," he mumbled, thinking of the way the Watusi had to be chased off the mountains whenever the guards caught them grazing their cattle off limits. But no sooner had he said it than he remembered that park boundaries are set by white people, and that for hundreds of years before the white people came this part of Africa was occupied by the Bantu whose only boundaries were tribal ones. Inside those boundaries the tribesmen had always been free to plant, to build, to kill animals. . . .

He was filled with guilt that he had left King and the others. Those apes were pathetically unable to take care of themselves in the face of any real danger. The poor old things couldn't run fast for very long; they could only climb trees, and King couldn't even do that anymore.

Sweating and swearing, he found that he was whispering prayers to—to whom? The Spirit of the Forest. "Please, Spirit, let them be far away from this place where bad men set traps. But if you can't do that, let the fog conceal them. Anyway, keep them safe . . . please, please." His breath was coming in sobs; his vision was blurred.

He was so crazed with anxiety and self-reproach that a strange confusion took place in his mind. The blanket of fog was not that at all; it was a moonless night— dark and heavy and filling his eyes so that he could not see ahead. He was back in Kenya. And this forest was not a forest; it was the farmhouse, its big black form sprawling like an animal keeping watch with one bright eye.

That eye is a lamp in the dining room, the only light in the house. And there is Father sitting at the dining table as he always did, with the two thirty-eights to the right and left of his dinner plate.

Something now makes Father get up from his chair and start outside. He slips the two pistols into the holsters he wears, and from the gun rack in the hall he lifts the twenty-gauge shotgun, which he carries in front of him.

But why does Father go outside at night, away from that one bright watchful eye? *Why?* Because a servant has told him that one of the "boys" is outside with a message about his son who is off on a little hunting safari with Njoroge. Trusted servants have ways of getting their bwana outside at night—luring him into a waiting trap. And what a fine trap that would be.

"Don't trust him, Father! It's a trap! Njoroge and I are all right." Jeremy tried to cry the words through his aching, burning throat as he ran blindly through the fog. Only it was not the fog that was filling his eyes, but the foreboding dark of a Kenya night. And he was running across his own pasture: afraid . . . afraid . . . and crazed with anxiety about what he would find. And with self-reproach, too.

"My fault. All my fault. I only hope I get there on time."

Get where on time? To the gorillas or to Father? It was all the same sobbing, straining need to hurry. Because now it was King who was feeding; it was King who was unaware that treacherous natives were lurking in the fog, holding knives in their hands and murder in their hearts. And King had come to trust one human the way the bwana Jenkins had once trusted his houseboy, his cook, his headboy.

"I lured King into danger and then left him to face it alone. King trusted me so well that he won't know enough to run for his life."

Nothing to do but keep going. And pray. "Please, Spirit, let them be far away; let the fog conceal them; keep them safe." He tripped over a root, went sprawling, and lay there without getting up, his face buried in the soft earth. A thought was working its way up through his consciousness:

I wonder . . . I wonder if, in that split second before—before oblivion, Father had time to pray to his God: *"Please, God, let them be far away from this place where evil men set traps. Or else let the night conceal them. Keep them safe."*

Father would have prayed. He would have if he could have. And he would have prayed for my safety, not for his own soul or anything for himself. That's the way he was, looking out for me—

"Oh my God!" cried Jeremy, sitting up, stunned by a new and horrible realization. "Do you suppose— what if— Oh lord, *yes!*"

Father knew better than to get himself trapped that

way. Why, even when we were at dinner and the house-boy knocked at the dining-room door to come in with food or to clear the table, Father would unlock the door, then make the boy wait until he was seated again with the two pistols pointing at the door. *Then* he would call for the boy to enter, not before. Father didn't trust any of them. None of the English farmers trusted their servants. It just made sense, that's all: a wise precaution. Also, the farmers of Kenya never left their houses at night. You weren't supposed to, no matter who was out there with what urgent message about your son or anybody else.

You simply did not walk through that door onto the veranda, not even with your two pistols and your shot-gun. You did not go out into the darkness: not in Kenya you didn't. Father went out there on purpose. He suspected a trap. He knew! But he also knew that Jeremy and Njoroge would be coming through the pasture any minute. (Remember it was after curfew.) So Father armed himself and hoped for the best. And he managed to shoot one of them, too. But there were others; and they jumped Father from behind.

After they did that they looked all through the house for the kidogo bwana who wasn't there. And they set fire to the house after cleaning out the gun rack. Then they ran, because they knew the police had heard that one shot, and would be on their way. And the stupid litle kidogo, whose fault the whole bloody thing was, is sitting here on the ground with his stupid little head all mixed up, and crying like a baby because his life was saved by his father and he doesn't even know what his stupid life was saved *for*.

He beat his fists on the ground. He beat his forehead on the ground. He gave himself to near-hysteria until he was brought back abruptly to sanity by a weird sound which seemed at first to come from far away. He stopped and listened: listened hard.

There is a peculiar ventriloquial quality about the mountains, and it is intensified by fog. The peaks bounce echoes of sound from slope to slope, distorting both direction and distance as well as the quality of the sound.

Jeremy stood, immobile, straining to identify that unfamiliar noise which was not altogether unfamiliar because it resembled nothing so much as the baying of a pack of hunting dogs. It was akin to the excited, high-pitched shrieking and crying and barking that could be heard in the Highlands of Kenya back in the good old days when one of the English farmers mounted his thoroughbred and set his pack of hunting hounds to running down game.

The idea of a mounted English landowner cantering through the dense underbrush on the Virunga Volcanoes was too much for Jeremy. His dirty, tear-stained face broke into a smile. But what was it? Surely it was dogs. And they sounded as though they had something at bay, for the shrill cries were sustained and breathless.

His heart pounded. Where there was a pack of dogs there were men: not just a solitary lawbreaking poacher, but many men—a hunting group organized with dogs, and each man carrying two spears.

Now he noticed that without realizing it he had traveled so far down the mountainside that the hagenia woodland was left behind and he was in the bamboo. He must have been running very fast. Also, the fog had lifted, or did not exist here; for there was a suggestion of sunshine which reached here as a pale green light filtered through the unbroken canopy of bamboo leaves.

The carpet of leaf mold silenced his further progress along the trail. If there were men in this part of the bamboo forest they could not be anywhere except on one of the trails, or close to it. For once the buffalo and the elephant blaze a trail through the bamboo, that trail becomes the only path possible for men. But which of the many paths to follow? Take a chance, and follow the sound of those yapping dogs.

In time he found himself slipping down a steep path that wound around the edge of a canyon several hundred feet deep, with perpendicular walls dropping down to a rocky stream bed. This narrow trail had been scuffed by the sure-footed buffalo, but for a human foot it was treacherous. Luckily he was forced to slow his headlong pace and take care with his footing, for it was then that he saw the human footprints in the earth. Now he was tracking men instead of gorillas. What he intended to do when he came across the band of natives he did not know. But simply by being a white man, his presence in this forest would

164

carry authority. Or even better, he might be able to pass himself off as one of the fearsome spirits believed to dwell in this forest, and thus use their own superstitions against them.

Now that he had picked it up, the trail of the men was easy to follow. Also the dogs were still howling, and he thought he heard warlike yells, too, the sounds piercing the quiet of this place where the loudest sound was usually the gurgling of a stream.

The tumult took on a new dimension; another sound was added. "Some poor elephant's got it," he mumbled, for he thought he heard among the cacophony of noises the high shrill trumpeting of an enraged elephant. Still, it could be something else . . . worse.

He raced, panting and gasping, toward the source of the yelling and the yapping that sounded as if all the wild hunting dogs had gotten into a fight with all the hyenas in Africa.

Again and again he slipped and fell, tumbled and rolled downhill. Then he froze where he was as one sound, reaching high above the other shrieks and screams, struck at his heart. It was an unearthly wail that rode the scale upward to a high soprano, wavered there, and fell with a gargling throaty bass sob that cracked and broke off abruptly.

It could have been uttered by a tortured human in a paroxysm of pain and anguish. Or, if this had been nighttime, it could have been the high despairing wail of a hyrax. But there are times when a sound is a premonition of tragedy: when it congeals one's blood with a certain physical knowledge that one's mind is forced to deny. And so it was with Jeremy, who set his teeth hard and tried to shut his mind to the awful suggestion of that croaking throaty wail, half human, half animal.

At a sharp bend in the path his worst fears were shockingly realized. There lay King on his back with the shaft of a spear protruding from his chest, the blade having gone in out of sight. King's bright brown eyes were shining with an amazing luster; and their expression was inquiring, as though he were about to put to Jeremy some question in a human language. Both of King's hands were clutching the shaft of the spear, holding it tightly as if it were a precious object that Jeremy might try to take away from him.

Jeremy and King stared at one another, communicating soundlessly. In the luminous brown eyes was the bewildered questioning; in the blue eyes, agony. Boy and beast stayed thus for a long minute, locked in silent communion. Then King frowned heavily, giving his black visage a somber, brooding, and melancholy expression. His frown gradually faded into a vacant glassiness, and King died without uttering a sound or moving a muscle. The life simply drained out of his body like the blood that was soaking into the black, loamy soil.

Jeremy whispered something softly to himself: "So that's the way a man dies." He forgot for the moment that King was not a man—forgot the dense pelt and the long teeth, seeing only those brown, forward-directed, manlike eyes with their luster of inquiry: the unspoken and unanswered question that stood between the two intelligent primates as they looked together upon the mystery that is death.

Then, still in an awestruck trance, he added, "It must have been like that for Father."

And at that point Jeremy's not-too-clear thought processes slipped into place a missing piece—fitted that piece into a blurred photograph imprinted on his sensitized mind one fateful night in Kenya.

"Just like Father," he continued, thinking that Father, too, was unable to frame a last question in anything more than a long, inarticulate glance: a glance that his son was too far away to see.

And in some peculiar way, that soundless communication shared by Jeremy and the wounded and dying gorilla satisfied a deep need—unrecognized until this moment, but one he had been carrying with him like a burden: the need to share a final farewell with his wounded and dying father.

Thus it was that one of Jeremy's private ghosts was laid to rest, stilled forever behind the closed eyes of King the gorilla.

But there was another. Jeremy was more than ever convinced that he was fated to be always just a little too late to prevent a killing. Death seemed always to be dancing a few feet ahead of his footsteps. It was happening again farther along the trail.

Several hundred feet ahead of where King fell there was a scene of furious confusion. Four young Africans, having dispatched the troop's only defender, were amusing themselves by beating the four female gorillas over the head with clubs. And laughing at them.

There was the baby lying where it had fallen from its mother's back. And there were dogs, about ten of them, with their teeth bared. They were snarling and growling and making quick thrusting and snapping motions at the gorillas' legs. And the poor gorillas! They were making no attempt to move away from the blows being rained on their hard little skulls, but only put their arms over their heads in a vain and pathetic effort to ward them off.

"Mur-der-ers!" he screamed.

All motion stopped abruptly. Clubs were poised in mid-air.

"Bloo-oo-deee mur-der-ers!"

His body was bent double with the effort. His face was contorted and suffused with blood. He knew what it meant to "see red," because for him the scene had an unreal quality bathed in a pinkish color. It all harkened back to a similar scene that had been lit by the rosy glow of a burning house.

The eyes of the four Africans bulged with incomprehension, then with disbelief at what they saw—or thought they saw.

Astonishment was followed by fear: the sort of fear that comes only from the bowels of men who have borne witness to the supernatural. Here was sorcery—being done with curses in some outlandish language. And curses can kill.

It took the Africans but a few seconds to call off their dogs and go racing single file down the path toward the bottom of the mountain. The bamboo forest took back its quiet, and a nearby stream gurgled.

The females crowded around Jeremy. Jack and Jill came down from the heights of the bamboo. They were all there, and they seemed none the worse for their experience. There was only some blood.

He took them back to where King's body lay, and

they looked. There was no sorrowing, no mourning for a fallen leader, comrade, mate. The gorillas stood about tentatively and simply stared at the lifeless form that was oozing blood on the ground. And their manner expressed, if anything, mild curiosity mixed with uncertainty as if they did not know what to think of it. Nothing else showed in those expressive eyes that contained a whole range of gorilla emotions but lacked the one called grief.

They looked at Jeremy then, and he realized that the pathetic little group of females and young, lost and bewildered in their abandonment, were turning to him for leadership. All eyes were upon him as if they were waiting to be told what to do next.

"Why—" he said severely, intending to ask them why one of the adults could not take charge of the group. But he knew why. What do they think I am? One of those young males like the ones in the other troop? He spoke to them: "I'm not a gorilla, you know." Their gaze remained steady, with a patient expectancy, a waiting, their always sad visages sadder than usual. And he answered his own question with the recollection of how readily they had taken him into their midst, fitting him in, as it were, to a clearly vacant place in the troop structure . . . of the way the old Queen, with her always sorrowing eyes, had glanced at him shyly with something like contemplation, or consideration, as if she were sizing him up. So wholeheartedly had these animals accepted his presence among them that it was possible—yes, probable

—that they mistook this creature they found in the forest for a lone wandering male gorilla, one separated from his group—an adolescent male ousted, as some are, by a jealous troop leader.

Well, he thought, I am indeed an adolescent male, and I have indeed been ousted from my group. That makes me a maverick, a rogue, like any other lone wandering animal separated from the pack, the herd, or in my case, the tribe.

Even so, I am not their kind of ape. What in blazes am I to do with them? These . . . these *dependents!* Why, the poor dumb things can't even forage unless King shows them where to go. They never move until King moves first. They don't start building beds until he starts. And they don't even know enough to run from danger unless King gives the signal to run. How about the way they just stood there, allowing their heads to be bashed. . . . Without a leader they're as helpless as babies!

He left King's body where it fell on the trail, giving it to the hyenas and the leopards in the manner of the Kikuyu. But first he covered it with bamboo stalks and leaves, which seemed a fitting thing to do.

That done, he led the way and the others followed, single file. It was a forced march. Up the narrow trail that wound around the edge of the canyon, along sheer cliff walls and up steep inclines slippery with leaf mold.

They responded well to his constant encouragement. If anyone fell behind he went to the end of the line and pushed. Otherwise he pulled. When night came they all built beds; at daybreak he urged them out again. There were no more of those lazy mornings, nor was there any of that leisurely wandering punctuated with frequent rest periods, sunbaths, naps, or other indolence. There was no frolicking play, nor any of that fussy picking and choosing of edibles. They ate as they went, lingering only once on one of the ridges when they happened upon a tree that resembled a large oak and dripped with fruit that looked like oversize cherries. Here they all stuffed themselves, with their leader filling his knapsack for later.

Their simple obedience was touching. He even got them to cross a stream after he built a bridge out of the heavy stems of tree ferns, and showed them by example how easy it was. "Bully for you. That's it. Good girls. Here, give me your hand; now keep going."

The four females showed a lot more stamina and fortitude than he had given them credit for. Even the new mother forgot to whine, and her baby did not cry. Jack and Jill had developed a new, more mature sense of responsibility during his absence; or else they were aware of the seriousness of the occasion. The behavior of all bore out what Jeremy had noticed: that a gorilla troop takes on the personality of the leader, whether aggressive like the big troop on the far mountain or permissive like this one. But never, he wagered, had there been such a leader as he.

"You're wonderful. Keep it up. Not much farther. Good show!"

He did not feel as enthusiastic as he sounded. What

if his charges were not accepted into the big troop? What if the young males were indifferent or the other females hostile? What would he do then?

"Get along there, and look as pretty as you know how. Gotta get you four girls married today—or at least betrothed." He tried to soothe their nervousness —and his own—with a running stream of comment. "I hope this works out—that it will be all right."

And it *was* all right. "To each his own," commented Jeremy when he saw Jack and Jill accepted immediately by the other youngsters; when he saw Queens Two and Three and the new mother come under the interested protection of the two black male gorillas, who snarled at the belligerent females-in-residence, forcing them to keep their distance.

Queen One did not mingle with the troop. The old female sat apart from the excited family circle, looking on disconsolately. And Jeremy sat with her. She had been visibly frightened when the silver-saddled leader beat his chest and screamed at Jeremy.

"Be gone," he was clearly saying, as he scowled from under a lowered brow. "You don't belong here."

"A fine pair of leftovers we turned out to be," Jeremy said to his companion as the troop ambled downhill and out of sight. "A couple of misfits, that's what we are."

He placed one of his own hands lightly over the gorilla's wrinkled black knuckles. "Look at this white skin of mine," he said with disgust. "I can't change that. Nor these blue eyes, either. I called myself an

African but I never was one." He rolled over on the ground and buried his face in his arms. "I wish somebody would tell me where I belong."

If he were an African he would have numerous kin, a clan, a tribe—all of which are family. If he were an African there would be rules about everything, every phase of a person's life, worked out over centuries of living. And he would pass in an orderly sequence, without turmoil or indecision, from child to young warrior to married man to respected elder.

An African of his age would already have passed through his several months of instruction. By this time he would have gone through the rites of initiation, a ceremony that would include all the boys in his age group, most of them his close friends. And those rites of passage would be the climax of his life toward which all his training, up to now, had been directed.

If he were a Masai he would now be facing the supreme test of courage: killing a lion with only a spear and a dagger. If he lived through that ordeal he would pass from boy to man. He would be a junior moran, a young warrior assigned to guard the Masai herds and join in cattle raids.

Jeremy, lying on the grass, thought about this thing called manhood and the way tribal boys are carefully prepared for it but white boys are not. Njoroge and other Kikuyu youths he had played with all his life doubtless had already been circumcised by this time because this was the year of their *nkumbi:*

First, the preparation. In the bachelors' hut, away

from the women and girls and children, the elders stay with the boys. They stay for months, telling the boys all the carefully guarded secrets of the tribe, secrets known to no one but the men. This is the initiation. After that comes the four-day ceremony, the most important ceremony in a tribal boy's life. The youths walk beneath an arch of sugar cane. Then the Kikuyu elders mark the bodies of the boys with white chalk to signify death and rebirth as a man. Then the elders face toward the sacred mountain, Kerinyagga, raise their hands, and call down upon the boys the blessing of Ngai.

The ceremony is awesome to watch. Especially the part where the boys swear a solemn oath to put the good of the tribe before their own safety at all times, and another oath never to reveal to anyone the tribal secrets they learned during their time in the hut. These are the rites of passage.

Then comes the dramatic climax. In unison the boys give one furious yell and throw their wooden spears over the top of the sacred tree. This is a symbolic gesture indicating that they have finally passed from childhood to manhood. For those wooden sticks are no more than childish toys, make-believe spears. In the old days before the British outlawed spears for Kikuyu, the wooden stick was replaced with a steel spear for each boy. But no more. Still, the ceremony of the spears was kept and it still signifies the end of childhood.

Yes, by this time his Kikuyu friends were men.

They had been given all the privileges of adult tribal members and all the responsibilities, too. And now, no longer children, each had moved out of his father's house and into his own house which he had built himself.

"Well," said Jeremy, rousing himself from contemplation, "I did that much anyway. I moved out of my father's house and into my own." He smiled a crooked, rueful smile and looked around at the forest which was like a house, with its green canopy roof and its soft grass floor.

A melancholy possessed him as he sat with his chin on his knees, his gorilla companion sitting motionless nearby. He was feeling low, and at the same time restless. To relieve his restlessness he stood up, took his sharpened stick, and tossed it as high as he could. The stick sailed over a little sapling and stuck in the ground. Then he sat down, feeling better.

After a few minutes of brooding silence he let out such a whoop of excitement that Queen One jerked away in alarm and crawled farther from him. Springing to his feet he cried:

"Y'know what? I've done it! The whole blooming thing! And the curious part is that I ddn't even know it! The preparation. That was all this time I've been in this forest. And in the cabin—like the bachelors' hut, y'know? The only difference is I was alone, but I learned a lot there.

"And y'know what else?" His eyes shone with triumph; he spun his body in circles. "You know those four men in the bamboo? Did you see the way I scared them off? They had spears. They could've killed me as easy as anything. But I didn't cut and run *that* time, did I? You bet I didn't. I just faced them down, like this—" He pulled a grotesque face. "Talk about killing one old lion, and with a spear and a dagger! What I did, didn't that take as much courage?" He paused for breath, exultant.

During this wild recitation, Jeremy's patient gorilla companion was gazing fixedly at his flushed countenance and waving arms, and listening with mild astonishment to the novel noises he was making.

"Don't you see, Old Funny Face? I've passed the test!"

He had to tell *some*body, and who else could he tell? To whom could he say: "I put the good of the tribe before my own safety."? What if they were to ask: "What tribe?" And suppose he were to say: "When the leader fell I took charge of the troop."? Somebody would ask, "What leader? Which troop?" He would simply have to answer, "I swore a solemn oath never to reveal any of the secrets I learned in the hut." That answer would be accepted by anybody.

But nobody is going to ask, he said to himself; nobody is ever going to know anything about it. I have to keep silent about all this because it would not do— no, it would not do at all for any of those crazy natives to find out that there is nothing to fear from either the gods or the gorillas that live on these volcanoes. I'll leave those fears in their superstitious hearts by keeping my lips sealed.

So, with upraised hand, Jeremy took a solemn oath: never to reveal to anyone the events that took place on the Virunga Volcanoes; never to mention to anyone that he had even *seen* a gorilla or had knowledge of their existence. (*They do not exist except in imagination.*) And Queen One was silent witness to that oath, spoken in the Kikuyu language.

The oath concluded with: ". . . and if I ever break this oath, may Ngai himself reach down from Kerinyagga and put a curse upon the gorillas of the volcanoes."

There. That ought to seal it. But he had to make certain.

There was no goat to slaughter, and even if there had been one he needed to give this blood oath as much importance as possible. So he took his knife, slashed his finger, and dripped blood in a circle around his feet.

With that, he patted the old gorilla on her bristly gray head. "Don't fret, old girl; living alone isn't so bad. Gives a chap a chance to think and to kind of figure things out."

Queen One, who had been leaning on an elbow watching the peculiar goings-on, gazed up at Jeremy with something like adoration, those bleary, sorrowing eyes of hers watering again. But this time, so were Jeremy's own.

That night he did not make a bed, but sat on a high cliff from where he could see, some ten miles to the west, two bright patches of red glowing like beacons against the black sky. He knew they were the two active volcanoes, Mount Nyamuragira and Mount Nyiragongo. But to him they were steady, timeless sentinels keeping watch with eternal vigilance—guarding these mountain slopes and all the wild protected animals that lived on them.

Ten days later there was a flurry of excitement at British Military Headquarters in Entebbe as there came limping up to the crisply efficient executive offices a sunburned towheaded boy dressed in stiff, filthy rags and laceless, crusted, mildewed boots, his exposed skin covered with insect bites and old thornbush scars.

"*Hullo!*" exclaimed the major. "Bless my soul. What have we here? Upon my word, it looks like—yes, I believe it is—a British boy! And much the worse for wear, I'd say. By Jove! what a sight!"

It took several days for British Military Headquarters in Entebbe, Uganda, to contact the authorities in Nairobi, Kenya, and to receive a reply to their inquiry about this ragged young savage who gave his name as Jeremy Jenkins, his address as "The Beautiful Bloody Highlands," and who otherwise told them nothing they wanted to know.

Meantime, the British Army provided this bedraggled wild man with a hot bath, plenty of ointment, a haircut, a dentist, and a doctor who pulled thorns out of his face and stabbed various portions of his anatomy with needles, but who grudgingly admitted that, cleaned up a bit, this skinny little scarecrow was a lot healthier than most of the people he'd seen on this army post and that mountain air must agree with him.

When the reply came from Nairobi it was:

> Sorry for the delay. The person you have in custody was listed as missing, presumed dead. Due to the present emergency in Kenya it is impossible to guarantee the safety of any British Colonial in Kenya. Therefore we request you arrange transportation with London direct.

Then there was some more about Jenkins, being a minor, becoming a ward of Her Majesty's government pending final transfer to next of kin.

When Jeremy learned that he was to be flown to London and met at the airport by his mother's brother who lived in a place called Kent, England, where the snow falls all the way down to the grasslands, and where there are very few wild animals, he only smiled a secret, placid smile. For a certain wise little hunter of the Ituri Forest had taught him that a person should never become so attached to a piece of land that he cannot move on when a shift in campsite becomes necessary.

Besides, Jeremy had plans of his own. In a year . . . or two . . . or three . . . Already in his imagination he was back on the misty slopes, tracking gorillas, then trailing every gorilla family he could find and scanning each black polished face until he came to those faces for which he was searching. Finding them would take time, but on the Virunga Volcanoes there is always plenty of time.

About the Author

Lilian Gould has recently returned from a trip she calls "the dream of a lifetime," to the part of Africa where her story takes place. She became fascinated with gorillas when she was writing *Our Living Past,* a book on evolution. The mother of four boys, Mrs. Gould is deeply concerned with "the origin of instinct and behavior, the causes of violence, the process of learning, the significance of sexual differences, and much more —most of which is overlooked in school." A Philadelphian by birth, Mrs. Gould wrote short stories and poetry and attended writers' workshops during the years her boys were growing up in the large household in Devon, Pennsylvania, where she and her husband still live, with their teen-age son.

5

DATE DUE

DEC 14 '84			
JUN 24 '85			
SEP 1 2 '89			
JAN 21 '98			
AUG 1 4 '93			
OCT 0 7 '99			

GAYLORD   PRINTED IN U.S.A.